I0589859

ON THE SUNDAY,
SHE CREATED GOD

Kara Sevda Press
Brunswick East
Victoria
Australia

www.karasevda.com

@karasevdapress

Literary Zine available soon.

ISBN - 978-0-6485118-4-7

In honour of all my teachers.
For my deepest and most despairing loves.
To Zane.

SONDER

New Year's Eve always reminded me of being in the bush as a kid.

I once rolled a large rock on its side. I watched the sentience underneath scatter into survival mode, shocked by my sudden presence.

Worms twisted themselves into knots searching for a fraction of the familiar dark, searching for a corner to writhe with their sightlessness, like kids on MD.

Bird calls scored the forest. Percussion came down from the canopy in shades of verdure.

Time is a wicked torch light that interrupts your own struggle in the dirt to show you that life is prevailing everywhere; even when you don't care to see it.

ONE

A city's worth can't be determined by the market value of its most elite suburbs, it isn't measured by the weight of A-class drugs waiting in empty parking lots and alleys. It's harder to pin. It's a simple matter of what's the city in your eyes doing? Laying down inviting you to consume its wealth and affections in carnal bliss? Or is this city leaving you without a pot to piss in, in its belly full of synthetic stars? Is your view from a rooftop poolside like me? Or through a dirty window? In this case the rooftop I was on, belonged to Owen Oprey of the Opreys. I liked to think the O in their name stood for old money; old house; overseas all the time. The sunset began to turn the skyscrapers into gold monoliths in the distance. The only time I'd be atoned to the sun was at sunset. I felt at home in the shadows like those clandestine worms. Staring into the face of another year, I'd let the smallest of experiences pass me by. Move around me as though an inconvenience, I was privy to the circular patterns of dark and light. Black shapes waltzing on the crumpled bed sheets, depending on how high the sun climbed. Sometimes it rained, sometimes the blue and red sirens cracked me open from inside my reverie, sometimes it didn't. Sometimes I slept and sometimes I left my bed for food, or a cigarette, a drink across a sticky bar and the races blaring. I swapped my bed for a park bench but only for a while. Sometimes I'd encounter a man, a woman moving their mouths and I'd occasionally try to grasp a word or two. Bit by bit you let the smallest of things escape you. You ignore the synth of the cicada, discarding their shells on eucalypts, with the hope to grow elsewhere. The sky washes over you leaving nothing but a story and the occasional warm body, but most of the time it's just you and that screaming alarm clock. I found it fundamentally disturbing I'd cheated myself out of common experiences, I'd never gone away or travelled, never drank wine in another country, kissed someone I truly loved. I never even touched snow. It was so simple and yet I'd never done it. Snow represented how I'd chased career instead of living. Snow was not just snow, it was a life of sunken steps.

Understanding the difference between scraping the side of the freezer with your fingernails and touching snow meant nothing to others, in life. And yet the curiosity and melancholia I felt about it moved me, into spiritual aggression. I wanted to burn the candle at both ends. Whoever first said that didn't understand how fucking good it felt to be dead and alive; to punch in, punch out till you're high on life, how good it felt to fight till you've got nothing left to prove. How good it felt to fuck someone till they're amorphous in your fluid, and finally how good it felt to feast till you lay that healthy turd the next morning. The delicious pain of being truly present — that was what I wanted; it was what I had been chasing. I wanted to be zero from living. But in doing so I had built nothing for my future. Now there was restlessness and another tomorrow. I wanted to leave, to go somewhere cold, pure, somewhere with foreign bed sheets and snow. It felt like it should've happened, like I was always on the precipice. Then just like that, you're sitting at a table somewhere, or barely blinking and nodding with a cigarette in your hand; fleshed into a hundred other moments of your own making.

This sunset, this view of this city had a lens of familiarity. The joint I lit began to smoulder its mossy smoke down my throat as the LSD created heat from the back of my eyes, projecting images. It was all starting to make me feel at ease. It was beginning to move parts of my mind around like heavy furniture. I began to feel the forgotten details that made this body a home, time began to slide away. The bruises on my legs were like dents on the floorboards where chair legs rested for years, the vibrant patches of wallpaper once shielded from light, were secrets only I knew. The places where dust had settled in some corners and that was what defined a peaceful space.

The lights blinked on. The rooftop was surrounded by fairy lights spread from potted tree to potted tree. Owen appeared and was refilling drinks for a group of people who were sitting gently chatting, their feet hanging near over the rooftop edge. Owen was the favourite student of all my favourite university lecturers. He was a person you're glad to have met but will likely never truly know. He looked at you while you spoke with an intensity that made you feel uneasy or desirable. He was finding tiny contradictions with your ideas, with an intensity which was really a mental dismantling, he may or may not share with you. His friends were upper class, bohemian and beautiful. There was nothing offensive about them, but that was exactly what was so offensive. They were the well-versed leftist progeny of the conservative who tickled their tongues with caviar while they talked about politics, and how 'those' hopeless bastards have managed to 'fuck everything up'. Their darlings were smoking a small part of their inheritance with the best ice in the city out of a Swarovski Johnson.

These people didn't like me. They obliged me and behind the smiling eyes of Owen's female friends I thought I could see them evaluating me and weighing up if Owen would ever fuck me. They'd never suspect I was weighing up the same thing. Particularly 'Box Hair Braids'. She and I kept accidentally making eye contact on our way to the snack table. We'd once engaged in conversation when I mentioned I liked a song that was playing at the party, we were casually stuffing cheese and bread into our mouths. She said listening to Flying Lotus was like listening to modern Jazz. I mentioned a couple of songs from Aphex Twin I guessed would build rapport. We walked away knowing the only reason we'd both engaged was because no one else was really talking to us. I was avoiding eye contact this time. The cars smudged by below as though they were never there, leaving only colour and sound to prove it. I could see Owen's face emerging vertically from the stairs that lead down to the rest of the house. The terrace was mostly sandstone. It had a working fireplace that had a mantle full of pictures of Owen and his sister Cynthia in their awkward years. When I ventured two levels down to find the bathroom, there were a couple people that had already thrown glass bottles into the fire. I heard the crack of glass shattering in the heat in one of the rooms that had a man and woman singing and playing guitar on a bed with people sitting on the floor around them, smiling. Owen emerged to the rooftop. He was holding pillows and throw cushions.

Babe jumped out from behind him and yelled 'Slut', simultaneously clocking me with a heavily beaded throw cushion. Immediately I began to feel right again and slapped her away, defending my drink. I was loose and starting to feel good, like when your muscles click into a position they understand.

'Shit, Babe, good to see you bothered,' I said, grinding my knuckles through her short blonde hair. She'd recently cut it in an attempt to no longer look like a pretty nobody.

'Ah ah ah! Not the hair! Took me forever to not look like a boy today.'

She sat on the brick ledge next to me.

'Need a fucking drink.' She pointed to the drinks table, which was unattended because everyone was watching the final flares of the sun, already high-as-fuck. A couple of pigeons had gone to town on some pieces of bread on the floor. Babe yanked a lemon from one of the potted trees on her way. I saw her slice it up and put it in a couple beers while she tried to kick a pigeon for coming too close to the food table.

I met Babe nine years ago. Back then her name was Babel; it was the name her family gave her. *Babe* was just the name she gave herself when she no longer needed them.

4

'Babel is a cunt who is scared of life,' she'd say as she psyched herself up to do something stupid, like swim in a filthy city fountain when winter was emerging. She'd been taught the word 'cunt' was vulgar and so she used it regularly enough to not provoke any suspicion that she didn't like it much deep down. Sometimes she'd be passionately pointing out her perspective on a matter, sometimes just plain red-face arguing with me and she'd stop suddenly and say, 'Babel is a cunt who cunt learn to agree to disagree.' She used these third person mantra's to cool down or psych herself up, she was summoning the best of both names, it simply did not exist. This construct she envisioned, as she once explained was a combination of apathetic coolness and chipped shoulders. Good God-fearing, sexless, Babel - the real Babel - wasn't dead; she was just gagged and bleeding in the basement waiting for the day of her escape.

When Babe left home, she left behind her little sister. One afternoon she balanced a cup of tea and a two-dollar colouring book on my bed. We had made-up a tradition for finding these colouring books with badly drawn princesses at the supermarket and colouring them while we got blazed. She always left her teabag in and sucked it at the end. Often she'd mention her sister. How she missed her. Not her as a person, she'd forgotten who she was and she had probably changed by now anyhow. She missed the way she once read her old books in their make-shift linen palaces on their bedroom floor as children. Babe's secrets always felt safest with her sister… above anyone else, even me. I think her confession was testament to how we miss past lives and strangers… Time is the only thing which can palpably break your heart.

When their parents would go to bed, Babe would wheel the car out from under the tarpaulin and driveway out of the predominantly white, working-class neighbourhood to find a party. One day while we were colouring a malevolent-looking Cinderella, she asked if I could be her new sister. My hesitation and not knowing how to respond launched her into those low sobs that women cry. They were sobs which sound like they rise from somewhere otherworldly and deep, a place which knew nothing of footprints, or voices which offered no language or reason. We all had this secret place, an underwater cave inside us which was a gateway to somewhere private. The only sign of its existence was the tidal rise and fall of her clavicle. To bring her back, I told her that time is not linear even though we feel like it is. Eventually we'd all come face to face with things we thought we'd shoved head-first into a grave, including people. Everything comes back. The second chance we're taught is rare often becomes the third, fourth, fifth, sixth chance to manifest what we want. The past only felt like the past because of the way we were living. Numb to patterns. I didn't actually believe this when I said it. But it felt good to say it at the time, maybe believe it for a second. It also seemed to calm her.

When I met Babe, we were both the most desperate we'd ever been in our lives, and somehow, we did become each other's family in many ways. We became confluent despite where I came from and where she came from. I came from a place with barely any shop signs in English and neighbours shitting out condoms of heroin in backyards. She came from a place where people like 'us' were here to take their jobs.

Most of the party were beginning to burst up to the rooftop; it was dark now. The wind had picked up a subtle smell of smouldering candles and a hint of the city's garbage piled haphazardly on the sidewalks.

The music was getting louder, SoundCloud rappers where fucking up the bass and soaring over the talking heads. The pillows Owen had brought up were piled in a corner of the rooftop. It was the best spot to view the party and the city. Owen placed his bong-pride Benita in the middle of the sitting area for people who were too high and needed to chill out with some weed. It was named after his childhood hero. It wouldn't be long till a party couple would turn the cuddle puddle into a fuck-fest though. People who don't feel like getting it on relocated like sexually un-liberated party-refugees.

Public sexual acts at a party were okay. Competitively reviewing other peoples' ideologies, the latest budget, their stance on the church, or which Alexander Wang collection was the most punk in sentiment, was not okay. It usually ended up in passive-aggressive animosity. You could be sure that there was nothing safer from taboo than watching a girl who probably only started bleeding three years ago get penetrated in the open air by an amateur DJ.

The music was blending into a kaleidoscope of MDMA canapés and kamikaze cocktails thrown down the throats of the silver-spooners. It was power as real as the scratch of a folded note between your thumb and index finger. They were now overcrowding the rooftop. These were the people next in line for everything. They were the future custodians of the keys which opened up secret rooms in the city, hallowed by editors, politicians, and socialites. They were the inheritors of vintage guitars strummed once by a cultural icon, and cases of wine worth the deposit on a suburban home. They were the inheritors of all that is borrowed, exquisite, and balls-deep cool.

'Is what's his face coming?' I asked Babe.

'Suppose he'll be here before midnight but he's probably with *her*.' Babe almost accidentally spat out the LSD stamp she was sucking.

'Who knows if he can swing it?' We both nodded understandingly as if we were used to having inappropriate relationships with married men. We weren't. The truth was dating a married man was like buying a bird of paradise on the black market.

He was forbidden, beautiful, and not exactly charming dinner conversation outside a bullshit-style Sex and the City brunch. Their relationship had blossomed from a desperate attempt at saving a marriage; the threesome was a bust, but the twosome between Pete and Babe wasn't. My eyes moved over to the palm nearby which had a group of guys sitting on the pot's edge and blowing bong smoke into a Persian cat's face.

'I mean his wife hardly talks to him. They definitely don't fuck, not since they were newly married at least.' Again we uniformly nodded as we sucked on lemon wedges post-tequila sting.

'He's never gone down on women before! He says it's not a man's job.' She hooked the words with her fingers when she said 'Man's Job'.

Who'd a thought the creases of women's genitalia would be such a wasteland of failed masculinity, I thought. I played along, forming a well-defined V under my darting tongue; we burst out laughing from the way it distorted my face.

'Wren!'

The voice felt clear in the noise, like opening chords of a favourite song, familiar though long forgotten in a catalogue of hundreds. It was Theodore Henry, known to us as Teddy, and he was calling out to me. It was the first time I'd heard his voice in almost ten years. He was squeezing through the crowd around the dance floor. He pulled Babe and me in for a hug.

I cringed; my stomach had been cramping hard all day. I thought the LSD and booze would sort me out for the night but the pain was pushing through the narcotic fog.

'What the fuck, Teddy!?' I was swiping through his pictures in my mind. I'd stalked him a couple of weeks ago knowing his birthday was due sometime soon. Babe and I bonded all those years ago, for the first time by dusting flour all over Teddy when he passed out drunk. A process known as *antiquing*. He'd always drunk more than anyone else at parties, because of this he had a village clown reputation. There was an undercurrent to his drinking. He said the more he drank the more the glass became clear and mirror-like... so he drank more. He would stumble around, slur, occasionally pissing on himself much to their amusement.

'Aren't we all trying to forget we aren't on the Moon?' He once yelled at a car full of laughing hipsters who almost hit him. He was chiselled yet soft, quiet but charged. We treated him with empathy and flirtation like siding with the beautiful boy picked on for his uncool shoes. He was just the right amount of broken. Babe tried to disguise her attraction to him and seem nonchalant; what better way to achieve that than to sleep with the guy? She claimed she only did it to dispel rumours of his small junk. Allegedly she felt bad for him and took it upon herself to report back. She said he fucked 'suburban' and it was 'okay'.

I thought her description meant 'clinical', though I hoped it meant 'inhibited' because their chemistry was all wrong and he was more than just a conquest. What we desire and what we fear is often the same thing. The fear of failing or losing something before you ever admitted to wanting it at all in the first place left people like Teddy crystallised in a time I'd never experience again. He would never be mine. Sometimes it felt like some of us were just drone bees who had never touched the grace of pollen, only the chaos of the hive.

I had a feeling Babe felt that way about him too, though I never knew what had happened between them or why they didn't pursue each other.

'How the fuck have you guys been?' His volume was attempting to compete with the swelling bass of the music. It was getting closer to midnight.

'Please don't fucking bore me with that question Teddy... Shit, I don't know how to catch you up.' People always forgot Babe's brand of honesty because her stature and small features all calibrated her to be the perfect girl next door. Or the disposable razor. Her appearance would cause such an oversight because she wasn't beautiful, just small and ordinary. She'd lure you into forgetting how cutting she could be and sometimes unpredictably so. I loved that about her.

'You go first,' I said.

Teddy scratched himself as though he was trying to put the last fervent years into words. He blurted, 'I had a baby.'

I sensed his disappointment with the normalcy of the revelation.

'Congratulations!' Babe said with concern, maybe sincerity.

'Sounds painful' I joked, ignoring the need to point out he hadn't done shit in birthing the thing. I thought the wife would be floating around.

'Remember when we used to shot Chartreuse in your kitchen because there was too much of it at work?'

'Your staff ever bother to sell it?' I laughed.

'Did they even want to steal that shit?' Babe took another shot.

'It tasted like Satan's cum,' I added. Babe laughed as she tried to destroy another lemon wedge. The reality was, the only thing worse than seeing a pink-face man about to shoot a load into your head, was the feeling of that load filling your cheeks and awaiting you to silently swallow his deposit. Removing that taste of warm fluid which had been congealing in a man's testes, was only possible with flammable liquid, like Chartreuse.

Teddy managed the bar I worked at when I was still a fresh 18 year old. We'd shared a house of bartenders slash whatever.

Our laughter died down. Quiet was happening between us. I looked at Teddy and Babe, both their eyes were looking downward and they were smiling to themselves. They were back there in that house too. Morning beers, late night coffees, the smell of burning blunts on Monday nights and then the newly bleached tiles of the bathroom on Sundays. Sometimes we'd host parties which spilled onto the lot next door known as 'The Block' a neighbourhood still proudly dominated by Indigenous Australians, they were feared but were just trying to live in this world too. Late at night we would ride our bikes around our neighbourhood together. Riding under the glass eye of the night felt liberating, hands, no hands, grinning, in silence just the click, click, click, of the gears... Nothing would ever feel that hopeful again.

I signalled a refresh of alcohol to both. Teddy winked. I shuffled my shoulders past other shoulders, and mouthed 'Sorry... 'scuse me,' to strangers. Box Hair Braids was yelling into the sky: 'In the future everybody will be famous for 15 seconds.' She was being held from falling over the edge by an androgynous waif. Box Hair Braids looked me square in the eyes.

'Lauren! I 'ava Masters Degree in business and commerce!' I wasn't sure if she thought my name was actually Lauren or if she thought I was someone else. 'I can only get a job serving brunch and coffee... It's like where did all these jobs come out of, where people eat more than they analyse their lives with numbers?'

I wanted to engage but all that came out was a shrug. I was high and frankly more fascinated by her New Year's face glitter mixing with tears and mascara into sad Bowie-esque streaks down her face. Box Hair Braids stepped away from the edge of the building and came closer to the drinks table where I was standing. The bottles on the table looked as though someone had gotten bored drinking the same thing and just moved on to the next bottle. Wastage is a sickness procured by people who have everything and get nothing from it. Grey Goose, Makers Mark, Hendrick's. There was a bottle of Remy Martin. I filled three flutes half-way up. I launched my hands into the tubs which had the champagne in it. The good stuff was always at the bottom, so I dove till I couldn't roll my sleeve up anymore. My hand came back with a bottle of Perrier Jouet Belle and frostbite. I finished filling the three flutes with champagne and nestled the bottle in my armpit to take over. It was Coco Chanel's favourite drink. It was the worse combination of flavours but it got the job done. The volume in Box Hair Braid's voice had escalated above the music to a shrill declarative tone. She was still staring at me while gently swaying out of time to the music.

'I wanna have beautiful bi-racial kids with O, but a bag lady can't have kids... where would I send them to school? FUCK-ING O DOESN'T LOVE ME.'

People around the table heard her; some seemed amused to see the drugs and alcohol picking off the weak. The dance floor was heaving with drunks towards us. They were barely able to stay on the glass covering the pool, which appeared to be the designated dance area. The lighting in the pool made them toler-able to watch. The pool lights accentuated people's eye sockets and limbs, making them look like drowned souls inside a sap-phire flame. It was hypnotising to imagine they were really dead.

'... SSSO HAPPY NEW YEARS.' Box Hair Braid's eyes slovenly closed. She was done yelling, so I took my exit. I looked over my shoulder to see if she was still watching me and she was kissing the waif. Teddy was peeling the label of his drink, explaining;

'I own a shop now. Well it's not a shop really, but it kind of is. We sell baked goods and repurposed old crap.' He seemed happy to not mention too much more. People's laughs and eyes are the same. You just have to wait an extra three seconds to see the authenticity behind it. Pay close attention as the facade breaks.

'What?' He sounded uneasy. I tried to focus on his face but the air was getting thick and I was getting lost in it, weaving in and out. I found something to lean on. It was the back of an outdoor couch. The people on it seemed close and purposely unapproachable. The seating area they filled was a tangle of overlapping legs and heads leaning on shoulders in group assur-ance or a group high. It was full of youthful camaraderie. Like those days you'd sit in a footy field after school, splitting grass blades down the middle talking about all the bitches you hated and the boys you couldn't have. Time was divided between the stages of grass on that field. Summer hardened the blades into yellow hay, and winter brought it back from the dead, looping into spirals of abundance and neglect.

'Do you have any shit you can sell me?' Babe nodded, looking for an acid tab for Teddy.

'Just take this. Old times sake.' She stuck her tongue out demonstrating and he followed suit. Babe placed the tab on the tip of his tongue as though they were partaking in the most unholy of holy sacraments.

I could smell pine (or was it sycamore?) in Teddy's cologne. He could probably see the beads of sweat having a meeting on my hair line. My focus was like the aperture on a camera, fading to micro and macro as the conversation rolled on and I felt like someone else was in control of my mouth and I was daydreaming on another rooftop.

'Are you happy, Lawrence?'

He called me by my full name; it pulled me into being present. The question itself was too direct, it was too honest to answer in that moment, so I didn't. We were momentarily alone and Babe was making her rounds.

'I only ask because you were always so certain about where you wanted to be.' Maybe he sensed I was incapable of answering in that moment but I was searching for the answer when I accidentally got tipped into a fantasy. I knew it well. It was a combination of photographs I'd seen once and a reel of fictional manifestations I felt would soothe me at my worst. It was a collection of moments I placed in a peaceful and accomplished life.

One was a tabby cat stretching its back on a perfectly made bed; my published book on a vast bookshelf; lips kissing my laughing face; walking through a snowy field; a glass of wine overflowing into a warm pool. And just like that they were replaced by images I lived through and cared to forget: crying into Mike as he tried to pull away from my grip; the hearse leading the procession to my father's funeral through the suburb I grew up in; the relief I felt from seeing his coffin go into the ground; then there was the assortment of humans in the unemployment line at Centrelink; drinking bottles of cheap bin-end wine in bed alone and wondering how I'd gotten back here. Again and again.

'Pretty happy!' Teddy watched my smile slowly shake away in the night like the ink on an Etch-a-Sketch, waiting for me to fill it with bullshit animation again. How long had it been sprinkling for? The rooftop offered no coverage. My stomach was cramping again with nerves. How was there an entire party not noticing the rain? How long had I been cramping for? I looked down to try and catch a glimpse of any blood on my jeans.

'Babe and I are doing a road trip, so I will be.... all those things soon.'

He knew my trick, the bullshit Etch-a-Sketch smile trick. He kept his eyes on me, watching my polite smile fade. Did everyone know this trick?

'Have you seen these buildings from a plane before? They look like shiny trinkets inside an old jewellery box, a mix of old and new. Don't you think?' I didn't actually know if they did appear that way in real life. I was more referencing stock footage of New York I'd seen in films.

The corners of Teddy's mouth were accentuated by two deep dimples each side. They looked like two quotation marks on his five o'clock shadow. I saw Babe was on the far right of the dance floor, pretend shampooing her hair, her favourite daggy dance move. It was coming to midnight. Her eyes kept drifting to Teddy and me.

'Where are you going on your road trip?' he asked.

'I'm going to touch snow for the first time ever. You can come if you like?' I sucked the acid stamp in my mouth.

I wished I could shove those words back into my mouth almost immediately after the smile.

'Really? Thanks.' Our eyes were comfortable on each other for a second. 'I've touched snow before. Not that great.' I was amused out of my reverie.

'So how do you know O?' Not knowing how close they were I corrected myself. 'Owen I mean.'

'Agi loves him so it was a given he'd be adopted by us.'

'Agi?'

'Yeah, she's the woman child. Her name is Agatha May. Maddie loved the name before she knew about the crappy books.' He leaned on the same couch I had been supporting myself on. 'She's three.'

I was transported back to Mary Jane's and watching my ice cream cone melt on the asphalt in the heat as we waited for my father to turn up. On the train ride home my mother was either fascinated by urban sprawl, or she was hiding her tears by his no-show. There's a generation of pain out there; women who are wandering through the hot streets and craving shade, melting with desire yet peeling themselves raw like summer fruit to be devoured. A generation of women slapping five cent stickers on their garage sale souls; everyone knows the hardware never stays cause success means everything must go. And everything eventually does. With tokens of youth, the Barbie dolls usually go first at a garage sale; perky plastic with the right parts, for others to enjoy, to pull apart, to play with, to place into positions which were cruel or self-indulgent, sometimes both. The things that showed character like old books with library loan stamps and macaroni art cards... well those are destined for the rubbish heap because nobody cares for someone else's story, no one cares to know of other people's childhoods. But it all goes until all that is left is a for sale sign in an empty room, and that feeling inside. That feeling burning a hole through the tunnels of your intestines, making you aware that somewhere along this process, what you really wanted was never going to be accomplished. Not this way! Nothing was ever to be gained by bartering or throwing it all away even though you were taught that's what you do for love: you give it all away. The moment of mourning, the moment you cast your innocence away and peer into the contingency of sex and adulthood. The pain of clicking that lock free, the loss of promises for promises sake, the loss of untainted underwear and untainted intentions is a pain particular to everything else you'll ever mourn because there is no way of going back. Ever.

The instant you realise you're female and no matter what power you try to wield, you will always come second, is the moment you truly become a woman. How much you give away will hardly matter. Less will never equal more.

There are good men out there. And men with puffed up chests full of poison like arrow frogs, fighting in the streets proving it was the world which did them so wrong. Shoving their hardened cocks into life, forgetting about the lives they created, and more importantly the lives they promised. I hoped Teddy wasn't one of those men. My heart was almost certain he was though. And just like that I could see the pink pool of ice cream being eaten by black ants again.

'That's pretty cool. You sound like you really love her.' I wasn't sure who I was talking about when I said that. My eyes were on my sandals and unwilling to look up.

'You look really good, Wren.'

I decided to not make a joke about how I'd stayed up on YouTube last night till 2am, watching tutorials on how to make my eyes look bigger, till my data ran out. The kids on the couch were taking selfies; one of them looked back at my hand, leaning in on them with annoyance.

'Thanks. You do too,' I said

He shook his head. 'Really? I definitely think I peaked five years ago. You should've seen it.' He made explosion gestures with his hands.

'Me too! So weird laughing with you like this again.'

'Well, New Year's Eve is the perfect chance of regretting the forgotten.' Babe's head appeared.

'Holy fuck, it's almost next year. It's almost the future!'

People started to collectively count down. It always fascinated me, that primordial urge to quantify movement, to give the illusion that we were advancing.

FIVE...FOUR...THREE...TWO...ONE!
HAPPY NEW YEAR'S!

The music came in and I felt elated for a moment that another year had begun, then nausea replaced that elation. Babe swung me around and gave me a big, wet nanna kiss on the mouth. Babe and I hugged, she then hugged Teddy. Babe was handing out nanna kisses to strangers; some of them were overly-receptive. Finally, I hugged him. I felt the dip of spine in his back, his hard body, only for a moment. Fireworks shot up inside the sky like flare guns in a city of floating spectres.

What the fuck am I going to do? I thought, just as Babe grabbed my hand and began to push and shove through rings of people hugging and dancing. We were running down the stairs of the house. Babe's hand had mine secured as we elbowed our way through the crowd.

Past the full room playing drum and bass, past a marble room of naked women in the tub, past the fireplace full of broken glass, and finally out the door. Somehow Babe found a cab and we were about to take off when we both heard a desperate Teddy from the window:

'Where are you going?!'

Babe opened the cab door and yelled, 'To hell in a handbasket! Get in!'

I was touching the beads on the back of the cabbie's seat, trying to distract myself from the pain in my stomach and the high of my brain. I was concentrating on how the street lights we passed bounced off each wooden bead. The pain kept creeping through.

'Wren lives at Hibernian House, so that's where we're really going. We're just getting loaded for free first at that pricks party.'

'I tried to go to a party there a while ago but I couldn't get in,' Teddy said.

When we got there the world's most graffitied lift was stuck at the ground level so we took the stairs. I ran my hand over the paint covered walls as we ascended the staircase, a purple dog was smiling at me probably on drugs too. A skull was moving through a web of black. The walls began to pulse with the music getting closer.

There was a rave happening in the hairdressing salon run by the world's friendliest lesbians. The usual street art geniuses were getting their new pieces out in the courtyard on level 4. Hibernian house was falling apart. It was the crumpled love letter to a city which didn't care about the people trying to read it. It housed ex H addicts, new age ice addicts, artists, musicians, a tattoo shop, and an illegitimate IT software junkyard which was a cover for a hacker hang-out maybe. My connection to getting a room there was an artist friend named Samson who I'd known from The Gong. His fingernails always had paint in them; he was one of the few kind but cranky people I ever knew. He was a night-dwelling, wiki punk who smashed walls with cans all night and got up the next day to work.

Hibernian House was filled with roaches; it was never clean; the pipes were always leaking sometimes into succulents as big as men's heads. Part of our neighbour's roof had collapsed a couple weeks back and the talk on how, or if, to fix it was still happening on the Hibern group chat. The lock had been smashed in twice for us. We left it as it was now as a way of telling our neighbours we had nothing for them to take. Nothing with hawker value anyway. It was a completely legal and illegal, dilapidated commercial building, which though was once used for commercial purposes, was now used by undesirables. Knowing someone that lived there was your only way in to gain residence, and sometimes entry.

We were on level six, where I lived. We found my make-shift living room filled with footage of Fellini, porn, and old BBC operas spliced together while the DJ played DnB.

We were intermittently moving to the music and making shadow animals and laughing at how we can only make a dog when I started to feel sick again. This time I couldn't bear it anymore. I tried to keep dancing, hoping it was the acid and that it would pass. Something was wrong. I pushed through the crowd, through the hipsters doing nangs in the open kitchen, past the rats conversing on the balcony and through to the dirty bathroom I used every day. There were girls doing rack with the door open in the cubicle next door. An ocean of sick was brewing around the darkest pit of my stomach was building. First, the vomit came out in an explosive torrent of yellow bile, splashing my face. I sat on the toilet and the blood began running coarsely, down the side of the porcelain, so seamlessly and tranquil in the rising quagmire. It felt as though something wretched was being pulled through the mangroves of my intestines, heaving forth and trying to release itself through the pink baleen of my vagina. My mouth was open in a motionless cry. A mix of fleshy matter, bulbous and dismantled like a deformed fist screaming out in the heat of battle, started squeezing itself out from my cervix. Slowly moulding its freedom through my seizing canal. And then it sunk into the red oily water. I swore it was rising up along with piss and excreta I had unknowingly released. It was going to reach my haemorrhaging cunt. How would that little hole in the base of the bowl swallow all this? The red in the toilet bowl was alarming; I thought I had ruptured something internally. It was the kind of red you'd imagine from a carnivorous orchid holding itself open for prey or when the wound runs deep from a machete-hack or the pulsing hole of a knife wound. The red was almost blue, there was a type of finality in the shade, of true sacrifice, like a part of you is forever gone. It was the most sacred and violent of all reds. I hoped I'd fall through it all like the eye of a rusted needle. It felt like peace was a faraway place in a land of milk and honey I'd never taste again. There were thousands of diodes blowing up in my mind and wires which were curling in the engulfing flame. The panic was deafening. My body was beginning to reject it all and drift somewhere. Babe's voice and the music were pounding on the door, growing faint. I heard gossip and laughter from voices near the cubicle next door.

I was fading when I heard the flush. I knew that the water would be clear.

And I would be empty again.

TWO

I was alive but bleeding again. The sheets had newish smudges of red on top of the darker strokes. I went to the bathroom and a large blood clot was staring me down from a newly cut square of quilted toilet paper. New Year's Day starts with this, my temples contracting in a cold condensation, my body was attempting to exhume the toxins I'd subjected it to with jest and good intentions the night before. I loathed her, me, it. Whatever I was now. I relocated back to Sayed's bed; he was in NYC on business so I was staying with Babe for a while for peace and quiet. There was a cherry blossom tapping its branch on the window like an impatient librarian hearing the worried whispers of my mind and shushing me. I looked over at my manuscript curled into a tight scroll in my bag. I was always scared I'd miss something so I took it everywhere with me. But sometimes it felt like a burden and I wished it'd quietly leave in the night. There were so many edits that I had't put into my computer at home that if I were to lose it, eight months of random ideas would go down the shitter, and I'd deserve it. Often I worried it wasn't meaty enough, or long enough. I told myself it's not about the size of the word count, it's how you use it.

Babe got lucky finding Sayed, I thought. The art deco walls were painted with Ralph Lauren paint. The wooden floors were styled with heirloom Persian rugs creating an effortlessly bohemian lux place. They ate from bone china plates Sayed bought at Harrods and drank gin with vintage glassware probably owned by a beautiful young couple mid roaring 20's. Sayed was a second generation Lebanese boy, hard-working, educated and with immaculate taste, and it was a shame his family didn't care just because he loved cock more than Babe. He was charging Babe basically nothing for rent so he could use her connects for the best gear around. Sayed was more cashed up than God due to smart investments, so he enjoyed letting loose when he wasn't working a 60-hour week. His leisurely activities were always double tapped by his plentiful followers. They didn't know that the smoothie he grammed was sweetened with copious amounts of cough medicine an appetiser to his benders. His followers didn't know that the beautiful man next to him lounging by the pool was a paid escort for the day. He confessed to Babe whilst falling into a k-hole that he would often drop into a brothel during his lunch break. Though he found women sexually repulsive he hated doing rack alone. He enjoyed their stories, their false names and the occasional visit to hetero land with a lipstick blowie against the backdrop of gay porn.

The quiet of the afternoon was punctuated by the moans of pleasure from down the hall. Pete must be here.

My heart killed my sex drive. I was mourning yet another relationship. In protest of sex and all that is intimate, I grew out my bush to its full capacity; I stopped shaving all my body hair in fact. I imagined my hair growing in a razor rebellion, searching for light after years of denial. I had stopped sleeping with Mike for the final dormant weeks of our relationship. Nothing quickens the process of breaking up more than the lack of sex. The skinny but muscular torso that once opened my legs smoothly in one movement began to rust. His face was a handless watch, useless and blank. I began to hate him but I used him as an emblematic reminder that love could be.

When I felt his hard-on against me in the morning, it moved repulsion in me and nothing more. He'd once said that my family had made me a broken person and I'd probably never find someone to love me, like he was cursing something that was already written. I smashed a glass of wine outside a uni house party after he said it. The glass cut his bare feet.

Our story was made up of so many moments of harmonious discontent. One time Mike bought me a diamond necklace for my birthday. He doubled the price when I asked him how much he spent on it. I found the receipt while cleaning and I realised that you can't make it work with a man who tries to change your taste in jewellery, then lies about the price tag.

I started to look for my phone and my rolled up manuscript. A friend took a screenshot of Mike's new profile pic and sent it to me. It was of him and his new girlfriend, beaming with love for each other. My eyes lapped up every detail. Was I more attractive? Were we similar? After the jealousy subdued, I felt bad for them. The highs in a relationship that his bipolar created and the aching lows, that was what I thought I wanted but that was never for me; but maybe it would be for them. Claire was her name: unassuming, sweet, and malleable almost and likely to not despair the privileged jabs of a "tortured artist on a low".

I began to recollect a couple of details from the night before. I remembered sitting on the toilet, crying.

Spider-like, I was now gently kneading the silk of my story from the night before in the sunlight, gathering the loose strands and snippets caught in the warm breeze of my mind, then weaving it all together like a patchwork of misery. I remembered everything, as I felt that familiar stickiness between my legs and I reached for the tissue box.

Babe tapped on the door as I bunched a handful of tissues and placed it in my underwear. Babe entered wearing the uniform of a conquered woman: his shirt.

'Last night was bat-shit.' She arched her eyebrows and lay near me, her legs were hanging on the edge of the bed. The occasional waft of combined cum and sweat defying her over-sized linen shirt.

'Getting high with Teddy hey, what a turn of events.' I was amused by his sudden rom-com-like appearance. Babe's coffee was filling my hissing stomach.

'Right?'

'You told him to come with us to the snow.'

I'd not forgotten about inviting him on our trip of self-discovery... or self-annihilation.

Babe seemed quiet. No, withdrawn. I could always tell when she was making small talk to deflect.

'What's up, Babe? Petey pop's problems?' I turned on my side to face the window, away from her. 'Do you remember much of last night?'

She moved to spoon me. I was only too familiar with that feeling of drinking to make something go away. Then comes the strip-tease of lavender light and the day comes to find you and all the mistakes you've tried to smooth over by cleverly making the bed.

I heard her sniff. I shook my head and hugged myself into a tighter ball.

'I don't know how it came to this, it was only once. How could've I not known?' In films it was always clear with morning sickness, and announcements. There was always a beaming father and it was always so noble to sacrifice your body to this creature which will no doubt complete you. I was the picture of a ruthless conception and a toilet bowl miscarriage. I recalled the pupae's body. It was no more than a slithering ball of despair, now sucked through the tubes of the city's underworkings, eventually to converge with the saline ocean, forever dreaming in seaweed skin, in its painless purgatory.

I whispered the name of the guy who did this and it unleashed a torrent of shame in me. He was my recovery fuck. The first in a string of cum pearls that most newly-single girls subject themselves to. Dan Elmstree. He'd managed to screw every nasty IG model and wannabe wog princess at work. He saw me tear up about the state of my life on my way home after work, and we ended up sharing sips of wine from the bottle at Hibernian House. I told him that the filthy scroll in my bag was my completed novel. I had re-edited it sporadically for eight months now. Eight months became almost two years. I was changing my life on paper, with a fake-ass grin I confided in him. In exchange, he told me about his dad. They had a loving but competitive relationship, even when he was dying.

'So one day we were play fighting and I went to go grab him. The way he shifted my hand, I lost my balance and on my way down I grabbed the first thing I could: his colostomy bag, which I had pulled and pierced somehow. Shit was all over my hands, on him too, and OH FUCK, the smell of it was fucking putrid. At first we were in shock; but then he started to laugh, and then I laughed. Soooo I get that sometimes things are so fucked up that sometimes your reaction to smile or laugh is just the sanest. You know, smile through the pain and all that.' His head had been down and when he looked at me, his face looked drained to bring those memories to life again, even if it was just to recall a couple of frames.

'I wish I could re-write some things too.'

I let him seduce me after his story. Oddly enough, knowing his story was far more tragic than a confused novel and a shitty job; was somehow a crooked aphrodisiac. Or maybe it was that I had watched a man called 'father' die too, just like he did. In hindsight, he knew this was how he'd crack me: through narrative and tragedy in the light of tea candles in a broken fireplace. He stopped talking to me afterwards. He completely ignored me. His man-boy disciples would ask if he and I banged. His answer would simply be a smirk but that's all they'd need to confirm. I was another notch on his fuck-boy bed post, and he was another disappointment. Hardly worth the time taken to kick my underwear off. Yet I looked for his eyes in the dirty halls of that call-centre, between calls from brain dead geriatrics getting their kicks yelling at another customer service phone monkey. I wanted him to at least agree it had happened. I'd watch him pass on the way to his desk. I'd inadvertently started a notebook of illustrations called "Cuntstomers", a documentation of the horrid people I'd been forced to interact with just to pay my rent. I wanted to show him. I looked for his eyes in the brightly decored staff kitchen. I was now a commodity used, another warm body asked to leave, and another pair of tits asking to not be ignored. As if I wanted more.

'I'm sorry.' My tears were running down Babe's shoulders.

She sniffed. 'Don't be, I'll be sorry for both of us.'

We both watched the window for a bit, I felt loved by Babe's desire to unburden me. The cherry blossom swayed, and broke the sky up into shards of azure.

A beep came out of my phone.

'It's Teddy.' I read his text out loud, wiping my eyes, not caring about the smudges of black it was creating.

Drop in I found something for both of you. Also I have coffee.

'Can't believe he has a fucking daughter.'

Babe let out a 'ha' but I could feel it was aimed at my prowess at deflecting feelings, not because of Teddy's circumstances.

'He can come if you want, you know?' She was chipping more black nail polish off her fingernails with her thumbs.

'It's probably better he doesn't.'

'Do you want to face the world today?' She squeezed me.

'I have to eventually.' This was the key, I realised. Learning to live with the pain and then numbing it with friendship when it all gets too much.

'I'll get dressed,' Babe announced.

On the way Pete was blasting John Mayer in his convertible.

'Do you think we could put the top up?'

He ignored me.

'You like John Mayer, Wren?' I thought of that John Waters quote: "If you go home with someone and they don't have books, don't fuck them." My take on that was: If you go home with someone who has John Mayer music in their possession, don't fuck them or let your friend fuck them.

'Yeh, he's okay, I guess,' I lied.

When we arrived, Teddy was outside smoking. He was wearing the same mahogany Docs he'd always worn since we first knew him. He was a classic 90's man who could still pass as a 'non-dad', as Babe said the night before. I noticed the hairs on his chest were beginning to grey. I used to watch him get out of his beat up Corolla from my bedroom window after he'd finished late at the bar. I had learned the distinct sound of his car pulling up. I timed his arrivals with a trip to the kitchen for water just so I could chat to him.

'Do you guys want the grand tour?'

Fresh dough was baking; it was so much more than a smell, it was a feeling, like someone was looking after you. I read about this place in the Sunday paper, and had no idea the guy who used to smoke bongs by the bins at work was now its owner.

A couple of women wearing yoga pants and full heads of makeup clucked out of the way: 'So then I just said, Sandra everyone knows you can't get a decent coffee, let alone a cocktail anywhere in Bondi now, without being bothered by a bunch of horny back-packers.'

Babe greeted them loudly with a 'guten tag' and I mustered the happiest 'hola' I could. Babe and I laughed at their startled expressions.

'This room is for all the collector crap.' It was a white room with a library of records, and a DJ who was playing ambient breaks in the corner, sipping a cap. Teddy showed us down the hall. There was a room of tables and chairs where people were meeting for brunch and chatting. We sat in the courtyard. The garden was wild enough to look loved but unkempt. There was bamboo everywhere. There was also an abundance of mint and basil.

'Why'd you plant weeds everywhere?' I asked.

'They weren't always weeds,' Teddy smiled, 'I guess, they grew so fast it became more of a theme for the place.'

'Maybe people only think they're weeds because they can't be controlled when they're thriving.'

Babe snapped her gum surprisingly loud; it seemed to punctuate my statement.

'What could I get you guys from the kitchen? Anything you like... on the house.' He clapped once and rubbed his palms together.

'Bloody Mary,' I said. He assessed my current state for a moment which he followed up with a sharp wink.

'I'll make that three,' he said and, just like that, disappeared into the fray of the cafe.

'Think he remembered that I invited him on our road trip?' I asked Babe as he walked away and we settled.

She shrugged. 'I'm headed to Pukesville.'

'I'm getting too old for this shit.' I lay my head on my stretched out arm. I noticed Babe was wearing way too much makeup for a hangover; the black eyeliner highlighted her irritated and blood shot eyes.

Box Hair Braids came out with our drinks and a plate of wedges. Teddy was following behind her holding a box.

'Thanks Misha,' Teddy smiled, and the girl haphazardly mumbled something and left. He put a box down on the wooden table and sat down.

'Fuck's that?' Babe was perking up, shoving the rough potato wedge down her throat and glancing at a group of preppy men on the table next to us. Teddy was clearly excited. He was letting the tension build as he sat back with a smile and sipped his drink. He pointed to the box.

'That's just some of the coolest vintage cameras you'll ever find.'

'What for?' I asked, more to find out why we should care.

'The road trip. I thought it would be a great idea if we documented it with some of the cameras I've collected over the last couple years. Some of these don't work, but some of them like this one.' He held up an old Polaroid. He unfolded some papers which were sitting on top of the box.

'I've got a couple of ideas too, about what we can do when we get there.' I was nodding and smiling but something was bubbling inside me. The confusion of his interest and initiative was wearing off. He had no place here, he had his own life and now he was trying to escape it by hijacking our plans. I was watching he and Babe get excited, touching the cameras, looking at the plans. He made his choice. He left the house. This need to get away, this restlessness was not his to claim; he had a home, one of those warmly-lit windows you walked past in the suburbs and you knew there was someone waiting inside for the others to arrive. That life was his choice.

'What about Agi?' I interrupted. He must've sensed I was in shock about how seriously he took my offer.

'She'll be with Maddie. They'll be fine.' He ran his fingers through his hair nervously and awaited my retort. I bit into the pickle garnishing my Bloody Mary and took a swig so big I almost finished it off. I noticed how busy his establishment was. Babe and some guy from a table full of men were observing each other from across the courtyard, divided by a fountain which was waterless and full of Chinese Jasmine. Teddy went on.

'So I've figured out a way we can leave late Feb, early March. I've got a couple of routes on Google Maps printed and highlighted. I also did a bit of research and there are a few pages on bars and cafes where we could maybe find seasonal work, if we get in early enough.'

It felt like the sun was getting hotter on my skin and I was suddenly unaware of other people's chatter. I was getting ready to say something so my heart began to beat slightly faster.

'I'll pay for most our accommodation; you know? You don't have to worry about that. I know you and Babe are skint. It'll be my way of thanking you for letting me tag along.'

Babe looked at me like a child does to a mother awaiting permission for a sleepover.

'What's the fucking point of these cameras, Teddy? I mean, honestly, we have phones that take better quality photos than these pieces of crap.'

'It adds effect. I mean, shit, I thought it'd be cool.' He looked off somewhere else.

'Like a water fountain without water, Teddy?'

'What is your problem Wren? I mean, you invited me and now, well I don't know about now...' Teddy was getting thin with me. He continued to question and make up scenarios about the potential of 'our trip'. I let his words fall on me like rain on a tin roof, it wasn't touching me, I was inside looking out to him as though he was an experience I didn't have to partake in. His opinion was nothing. I looked around and I thought about the cool nonchalance of his cafe and how it made this place so beautiful and popular. It made his money seem so effortless. Everything had straightened itself out for him. He'd married 'the right girl'; the type of girl with the biggest house on the street, with the best Christmas decorations and a neatly manicured lawn. He was no longer a rat like me; humble, dirty and seething, fighting for every scrap, trying to gnaw through the aluminium frames of shiny new homes. He had escaped that single-parent, ripped fly-screen, scum-bag childhood we bonded over and I'd hoped we'd heal together. He was a stranger in those suburbs which we called home, those suburbs where the only thing that outnumbered churches were abandoned car lots and fast food drive-thrus. Places where you were told, 'Be careful of needles' when you went out to play. Places which were visited by politicians come election time; where if they shook enough yellow and brown hands they'd be ticked on the ballot paper. Places where the train line would not continue, road works were forgotten, yet blue-lit public restrooms were always open.

Those places were in his rear-view mirror now. I'd only taken sabbatical. To wish his new life away was blasphemous, but to slum it with us was as ludicrous as a double simulacrum. You had to earn the freedom that Babe and I had through suffering, and you could only do that when you embraced that it was handed down to you the same way I would've handed it down to whatever it was that released itself from me last night.

I started to leave but I tripped over some wooden table legs. The glasses on the table toppled over. My glass rolled off the table and shattered. Teddy was off his feet, quick to help me.

'Just leave it!' I screamed.

The cafe had stopped, and the table of handsome men were looking over at me with amusement.

It was written all over Babe's face. She was worried I had snapped, fully knowing what had happened before we came here.

Everyone was staring at me. I was making a scene. All I could do was run.

As I got up I promised myself to make Teddy a stranger again.

'Wren, wait,' I heard his voice call out, but there was no point in turning around, I had made my decision to go back to keeping the lamp on and curtains shut. I could lose myself in the glowing scroll of other people's lives, lose myself in the countdown till the next episode begins, the right or left swipe on a temporary love, the knock, knock, knock of food delivery. Another spliff lit, a couple more clicks, a couple more hearts to appear on my screen and I'd forgotten that I almost lived again.

TWO ½

'Hi Lawrence, so we have great news! Slate Advertising would like to offer you the position.' I looked at my phone in disbelief; I had The Drones on pause for this phone call.

'Are you sure?' Leigh, my recruiter, chuckled reassuringly.

'Yes. They loved you, they thought you were present, driven and would fit in nicely to the team culture.'

I had smoked a joint before the interview to ease my nerves so I was confused about the being present comments since I was so baked.

'They want me for the copywriting position?' I was doodling on the back page of my manuscript; a picture of a man whose head was on fire.

'No, they want you to start as an account executive, then they'll see how you go and maybe move you to the creative team down the track, you know, once they get a sense of your workstyle. So how does that sound?'

It sounded reasonable but I was reluctant to compromise with advertising folk. It was a slippery slope to be on because if I said yes, it would be a yes to being primped and prodded like a show dog by the Boomer and Gen X naysayers who created us. It would be yes to their fingers in the teeth of my experience, and filling out any cavities in my abilities with sound and aggressive mentoring. That's all good but can she follow direction? Can she jump? Can she roll over and bark on demand? WOOF WOOF I'd say with my rehearsed answers, yes, I can! I know I can, I know I can. It would be yes to a close inspection of my fur and posture to see if I fit into the beautiful world of advertising.

'Sounds great and look, I don't want to sound ungrateful but, Leigh, you know I'm a writer, not a suit. You told me you could get me writing work. Is there anything else out there? I'll do anything just not this.' There was a pause on the other end; she was gearing up to convince me otherwise. 'You know I only went for that job as an off-the-cuff decision.' My drawing had evolved into a full illustration of a man with a grotesque melting face.

'I know, but like I said it may be a great way to get your foot in the door.' *Not your commission?* I thought.

In fact, I had worked for an agency before, I knew how this worked. Junior staff members were clearly the have-nots and we were asked to smile while we munched on their daily intake of shite. The obsession with agency awards and their image always superseded the quality of work. The same beige slop was perpetuated while their buzzwords filled rationales and keynote presentations. They were the people in the control room of ideas for pop-culture. It's no wonder we were a gen-eration of batteries sold separately and cold mushy ethics, now served with less sugar and less preservatives. The product being sold at an accelerated pace was now you, nothing left had value. There were no labels needed anymore just individual walking brands who would talk to other walking brands, selling images to each other to profit in social currency. We would do the bid-ding on behalf of the execs, and all for what? We validated our-selves by perverting everything else; privacy, relationships, for a couple of double taps, a couple of clicks and likes, a couple more seconds for their pre-roll ads before watching YouTube for a couple mindless hours.

Our parents were so busy trying to give us what they lacked, they forgot to teach us what we needed. Television cued us to laugh, movies taught us to chase desire through airports and the internet told us to connect by staring at the marble camera eye or leaving your comment in the designated box below. We told ourselves we'd be OK if we played with our privilege. We invented new and speedier ways to be loved for what we could be worth, not for what we were. We hated ourselves as much as they hated us. I would've done anything to opt out forever; I clearly imagined me as a charred Lady Godiva riding through the streets with my unbrushed hair. I'd already drunk from the phallic teat of the machine. I'd had enough. It's funny what that sour serum does to your spirit once induced for so long: it gives you a title, a business card, and manipulates your palette to want more, no matter how much it starts to rot you or how ashamed you're made to feel when you no longer want it.

This is the greatest affliction of the western world; this divisive and granular resistance to self. The boardrooms filled with deafening silence before the anointed one speaks. The days are counted, till our booked holiday to get away from the drudgery. Execs are living double lives as agents of chaos in Black Rock desert where they'll be free to vibrate on noise pollution and narcotics. This is the power of paradox we are sold; self-importance and connectedness.

The days are counted and scratched into these computer programs like tallies on filthy prison walls; generations of misery taught, misery endured for a weekly wage; a sick competition of which snake may purge on its own tail fastest and be back by popular demand; which fool will be the last to laugh his spittle into the cold air. The world feasted on their daughters and sons, like Titan's, throwing their broken spirits and bodies into our homes, into our beds, our streets, expelling the sickest and poorest into wars the wealthy had become bored of. I didn't want anything to do with nine to five, with ad men, with the morally corrupt refuse we call work. I would've done anything to show anyone that I'm just a writer wanting to trudge through the burning garbage littered through our end of days. I wanted to create meaning through my vocation. I wanted to live creatively and report on my findings to people who still cared. That was never enough. There was always someone to outrun, someone to fear, someone to prove yourself to, someone to maybe even demean on your way through, someone's chocolate star to lick, someone else's hand to suspect will snatch the bread from out of your mouth. Being a creative full time was still a small club of the privileged here. No-one talked about what they had to become or what they sold in order to get it, no-one wanted a community, just a panel of gatekeepers and bureaucrats. But I had had enough of all this, I knew where that cannibalistic world begun and I didn't want to get lost in it again. Fuck having to get back into ad land just to be around some version of ideas generation.

'Leigh thanks for the opportunity but I'm not going to take it.'

'Okay, Lawrence, fair enough. I'm just going to be blunt with you now. You don't hold much experience. It's going to be difficult to get you anything, despite your education.'

'I'm aware. In fact I've been told that for a long time about everything.'

'Okay, I'll level with you more. Writing jobs are few and far between. You're competing with people who will do it free or for peanuts. Everyone can create content these days, most of them Lena Dunham-wannabe girls too.' She lost her patience with me clearly after months of saying no. 'You're not more employable, even if you have a degree because words are dying in the digital space, let's face it.' She kept going. 'Please consider this the golden ticket to making a decent wage.' I'd stopped drawing and was pacing now.

'Leigh, thanks for your help but I'd rather clean toilets.'

'Well Lawrence, if that's what you want, that's what you'll get.'

I knew she was culturally cursing me. She hung up. I looked at my manuscript, it was rolled up like the dirty bed of a gypsy. Its pages were browned and drawn on, a frivolous collection of composite faces and fleeting moments that resembled life. I'd edited several parts so much that I had to insert extra blank pages. I was avoiding retyping it because I was worried my good intentions and literary insecurities had maybe undone a good first book. I shoved it back into my bag. I was meeting my mother at the cafe down the street.

I saw my mother before she saw me; she was standing by the lights. I tried to imagine seeing her through the eyes of a stranger and seeing her for the woman she was. It had been unseasonably cold and raining. The wet asphalt was reflecting the colours of passing umbrellas and torsos marching on to appointments and meet-ups. My mum was wearing a long cardigan. Her hair had only just started to grey. Her skin was naturally dark; she looked like a regular sweet woman, like someone's mother. We shared the same body type: thick, and like we were built for a hard life.

'Mama.' I gave her a kiss and hug. I had to bend my knees to reach her face, she was so small.

'Hola hola, como estas?'

'Bien, bien.' My mother was from El Salvador. Her accent was still formative, even after years of being settled here. We lost contact as often as I lost phones, which was often. I found no need to be close to her these days, as I felt no need to be vulnerable with anyone else but my chosen family.

'How did the interview go?'

'They were fine, they offered me a job.'

'Mamita, why do you look sad then? Did you take it?'

'It's not the job I wanted.'

'You need the money; you need to think about your future.'

This brought on the typical daughter-of-an-immigrant speech about goals and making it good. The word 'compromise' was used a lot. Moments like this, my mind shifted through to a time when things like this didn't matter.

My Dad, Mum and I were happy sometimes. They both educated themselves when they came over; which meant we had to live in places deemed dangerous by real Australians. It was the only thing which was affordable for me and my immigrant family. They left when the revolution was rife with bloodshed and the illusion of a winner had been shattered. This wasn't uncommon. This was the Australia I knew. First generation, translator children, who'd bridge the language barrier between the living and the nearly dead. Between those who were raised here and for those who left everything behind. The kids with the exotic lunchboxes were my friends. We weren't represented much. We were often asked to pick an identity, whether we were born here or not. Proving your 'Australianism' to not offend was a well versed practice. We didn't celebrate with flags on Australia Day, we celebrated other things with more pride but there was not much room for other voices in the fabric of Australian narrative, not even for the first inhabitants. This was a place built on survival and violence. Cruelty was hard wired into this society. It was especially unkind to those who came here by boat or asking for asylum. My family immigrated here before Manus, but if it had been around back then, our lives would be very different.

My father was abandoned as a kid; he grew up to be a political prisoner; my mother, a runaway teen who was also later an active rebel militant in the civil-war. There were moments of real love, even peace between the three of us, though we were opposed diametrically in most ways, and none of us really understood peace. My parents agreed on few things. They shared stories of fallen comrades, the innocent people they knew to have disappeared.

My father worked to satisfy that consistent stack of bills on top of the fridge. My mother worked to calm that rage under my father's skin. She'd fail and it was often her, not me who would have the open palm to her face or the broken nose bleeding into a fistful of toilet paper. We were afraid of him and his viciousness. A question could trigger a storm of names, broken household objects, mauve patches blooming like clouds of ink.

The truth is it didn't matter who he'd hit, or what we'd say to conjure his rage. Mum and I were just constructs of the woman who left him to eat nothing on the street when he was a child. It would be easy to say he hated us, but the truth is maybe simpler. That kid, begging for food, sailing paper boats down sidewalk sewers, he loved that child in him so much more than he loved us.

Our family dog was the other bitch he'd beat. Sometimes she would pull the bed sheets into the dirt which were drying on the line, he'd beat her. When she ate his tomatoes and destroyed the vines for future fruit, he'd beat her. Even when there was no real reason; like when she'd menstruate on the concrete garden path, he'd kick her. His main tool was his shoe but occasionally he'd get creative and use objects like the plastic rod from the venetian blinds, or a remote (which he'd snapped in a rage). Her whimpers are something I'll never forget or forgive that dead fuck for. The dog would urinate in fear when she saw him, yet she still cautiously approached him for affection when she was called. I suppose I understood it because on occasion he was almost tender. He'd hold me when he came back from the factory; he'd plait my hair while I ate freshly cut oranges after school and chatted in Spanish. Peace was the mortar between the red bricks of domestic bloodshed.

My parents understood allegiance as much as they understood violence. That was the only thing I consistently knew of people. It was the interminable ability to absorb pain and come out intending to express love. Pain and love, they were the two faces of a coin. I knew early on you could watch it defy gravity for a moment while it flipped gloriously in the air but either side it landed on would lead to the other eventually.

We were standing at the counter to order.

'Can I please have an iced tea, jasmine please; and a large cappuccino?' My mum put her hand out to pay. She knew I was poor again.

'Can I have a name please?'

'Lawrence,' my mum smiled annunciating through her accent, drawing a circle on my back with her warm palm.

'Sorry, did you say Lara?' the waitress squinted slightly annoyed.

'No, Lawrence... like the boy's name,' I rolled my eyes knowing it was easy to understand different accents if you bother to pay attention, yet most monoglots expect you to say things exactly like them.

I asked her once why I had a boy's name. She told me it was because the nurse didn't understand her when she was trying to name me Florence; after her favourite city. One day she confided in me that I was actually named after my older brother Lorenzo who had lived a couple months. He passed of SIDS. She never talked about him. Except for once she told me that she always thought of him and what type of man he'd be if he were alive today. I wondered the same also. She said she felt so lucky to have known him; she had so much love for him she decided to bless me with his name again, but the Westernised version to avoid Latin superstition. She wanted he and I to share something.

'Death is impermanent, Mamita,' she'd say, 'and life always won.' So he was out there somehow living, somewhere maybe not as himself but something surely just as magical.

'Mamita, you're lost right now, but it's okay to be. You'll figure it out.' We walked down to the station where she was getting a train back to the inner-west. She was looking after some women for the afternoon shift at the drop-in centre. 'Do you remember when you wanted to move to Ireland with Berto?'

'Si, porque?' I sniffed. I was getting emotional which I hated.

'I thought, "She's leaving us." He was your first love so I had to let you go and watch you make your own mistakes. That's the hardest thing to do: watch someone you love struggle when you see them clearly. But I know what you're like, and you'll be fine. Aqui, yo lo se.' She pointed to her heart.

The station was welling up with commuters. I needed to put my jacket back on and the beautiful silk scarf she'd gifted me a while back. It got caught in the wind and was flying away as I tried to get my arm through an arm hole.

She caught it and in one movement she wrapped it around my neck lovingly and put her arms around me. I let tears soak through her woven green cardigan. I wanted to explain what had been happening with me but even if I could, I knew words would barely be able to comfort me as much as her instinctual, swift embrace.

THREE

A man's white tee shirt; two glasses of wine, barely touched; a couple of pairs of underwear taken off in-haste. The light was filtering through the holes in my curtains.

'Hey,' I whispered to him - 'him' being a guy I found at a high school friend's party. After I caught up with my mum I was restless. Hibernian was a hot house full of ghosts picking the dirt from their nails or staring into space with black phone screens. To get away, I often caught the train to nowhere for entire portions of my jobless day. The train would snake through the city and I'd listen to the announcements, the metallic itch of the tracks. Depending on the time of the day I'd walk through office workers on their commute or I'd walk through tourist's conversations, which always felt like a tease of exotic places. I'd get off and wander through parks and different streets and try to find somewhere new. I'd usually light a joint and stop in for an Irish Coffee (my stash) or vermouth on the rocks, depending on what hour I stopped my wandering. I'd let the world delight in drinking me in. I'd find purpose in drinking her in, and the idea that we are all the one moving piece. And I would write and write and write. Only stopping when my hand would hurt or because I needed another sip. I'd write nonsense, sometimes. Sometimes I'd write something and want to kiss the stranger beside me. Sometimes I wanted to yell it out, once I actually did. Sometimes I'd make myself cry and then I'd need a shot of espresso or whiskey, depending on if it was sunny or not. Sometimes I'd write on napkins just cause I felt like a fake, or worse, like all this didn't matter anyway. Sometimes I'd read my first rejection letter from Urchin & Eden. Sometimes the sky would burst from the heat and lap it all up again from the hot asphalt like an alley cat. The night would later cool, at times long enough to let the blades of a slow fan do it's bidding on condensed skin. I'd never tell people where I had disappeared to for hours despite the odd questions about where I'd been. I'd never tell them I was writing because it wasn't any of their fucking business. Being on the train made it seem like I was moving towards something and anonymity was part of the journey. The train was meditative: it made me braver, to enter the madness with nowhere to go. This gave me spiritual licence to actually attend an old friend's party.

I hadn't seen her or any of her friends in years, just the odd online catch up. After a night of no sleeping I looked at pics of their group holiday to Mykonos. I was the hundred and twelfth person invited to this blow out. The guy, who was now asleep in my bed, knew all of them, some of them intimately, of course most of them had slept with each other. Half of them decided to go look at glow worms in an abandoned railway tunnel, I thought "fuck it" and tagged along.

We stepped over train tracks and through large fern leaves; trembling hands of velvet reaching out to touch us in the night. The little green lights above messed with my earthly senses and I felt as though we were stepping through some celestial portal which would allow us to float with naked stars, reachable even in their glory. Naturally I kissed him.

He had freckles and blonde curly hair, his penis was now flaccid and satisfied. His bottom lip had a silver stud; he was the best looking by far. I didn't take my top off or go down on him. Letting him fuck me almost had the same effect on me as disappearing into a crowd at a train station or a portal. We were both elsewhere while inside each other.

'You should go soon.' I hoped that volume increase would make him stir. Getting them to gently fuck off was always difficult.

I moved through the mental memory of falling into bed with him, feeling his tongue in my mouth, then trying to awaken my clit. After the obligatory amount of licking was done there, I fastened my eyes to the flickering light bulb and felt the weight of his body on top and inside me, racing to completion; he was a stack of muscles converging, trying to create a moment, but only for one. I was laying on a damp patch with my back to him wishing he was someone else. I fell asleep listening to a playlist I made with songs which had some sort of instruction in the title, like "Don't Smoke in Bed" and "Don't Bother Calling" and others which felt like implied instructions like "Young, Dumb and Broke". We slept and woke up on opposite sides of the bed.

My phone started buzzing with the word, 'SLUT'. It was Babe. We decided to rip the word apart like old jeans and reuse it as a thing of camaraderie between us. The fact that it offended people outside our world was just a plus. We used it all the time. 'Pass the salt Slut, How's your day Slut? Love you Slut,' and just plain 'You Slut,' when deemed each other sexually successful. New wave feminism was about repurposing ideals anyways, and if other feminists didn't like it, fuck it.

It took me a while to send Teddy a text and apologise after the café incident. He barely wanted to hear an explanation about me snapping at him. He replied almost right away to my text, Teddy was old-school like that. No games, no grudges, just sincerity.

'Was just worried is all. I don't want to lose touch with you.'

I watched the ellipsis appear momentarily on the screen. Was he being careful how to phrase it all? How can three dots hold the weight of expectation so cooly?

'I mean... with you (emoji of two dancing girls) again.'

He put two girls down instead of one. Another person was playing in this space with us suddenly. We were alone but he opted for that extra couple of pixels to take away the intimacy of our conversation. I was a collective, a package deal, friend-zoned in the clearest and cleanest way. An emoji.

He wanted to stay in Babe's and my life. I guess when you're older you crave history with someone because sometimes it seems easier to mind map yourself with someone who was present before identity mattered so much.

I had been too ashamed to even contact Babe till she DM'd me about a writing job she knew I'd be interviewing for. We arranged to have drinks when Sayed got back from the UK and commiserate the Women's Health gig I'd never have. After a few glasses we got excited about the road trip again. We were on the same page. We drunkenly talked about the things we needed to get away from, when Babe put her hand up:

'Need to get away from Pete, he's getting me down, man.' Pete's wife had started to follow Babe around town. She'd spotted her mid-handshake for a deal she was closing for Sayed.

She threatened to tell the police what a 'disgusting little drug whore' she was if she didn't 'stay the fuck away'. I couldn't feel for a woman whose head and heart were at odds. Yet I did. The result of this less than desirable interaction was a parting of ways between Babe and Pete. She admitted to us, post shot she ended it with Pete more out of laziness than any kind of fear, kind of the reason why she never explained to him her real name. She didn't want the carcass of his marriage stinking her life up anymore. 'I've got my own problems, you know.'

Teddy and I both held back and conclusively said we just needed to get away from life. I had a feeling I needed to get away from some kind of death too.

So now Babe and Teddy were downstairs, probably in a fully loaded car ready to hit the coast road, and then Jindabyne to await the season's first snow. I got up and tried to find my underwear at the foot of the bed and in the sheets. I gave up and tried to find a fresh pair, but I settled for swimmer bottoms. I hadn't done laundry in weeks. I left him to stir in the grey darkness morning usually offers. When I got downstairs, Babe was in the front seat with her foot hanging out the window.

'Open the back.' I was half asleep and still drunk. I caught a glimpse of Teddy's face in the side mirror; he looked confused. His hands were on the wheel ready to go.

'Are you putting garbage bags in the car?' His eyebrows were ajar with confusion or judgement in the mirror.

'That garbage is called a wardrobe darling. I'll have to get on top of laundry; everything I have has been worn inside out twice. I've passed the skanky undies stage and I'm now down to swimwear.' I smacked my own ass.

'Ohhhhhh.' Teddy's brow subtly furrowed as he tried acting like he was less confused.

When I got back up to my bedroom there were urban hippies smoking the peace pipe collapsed on each other listening to Yellow Days full blast out in the makeshift living room, "A Gap In The Clouds" was blasting with joy through our corner of Hibernian.

'Wren, you want?' He lifted his arm holding the bong. I noticed the cone piece was loaded and it was ready to go.

'Sure. It can be a goodbye gift I guess.'

'So are you coming back?'

I tried to shake my head. He watched the cone I was punching turn orange under the heat as he spoke.

'Bummer.'

'I've only paid rent for a bit. If I'm not back by then, then it's up for grabs I guess.' I grimaced as I let the smoke back into the ether and watched it curl away.

'Cool, I like your room.' He was typing something on his phone.

The room really belonged to the roaches, rats, and the secrets I'd written in a sharpened lead pencil on some of the walls in states of highness on the odd occasion.

'I'll see you when I see you then, Hank. Thanks for the hit.' I thought he was going to hug me but he held up the bong next to me and did a shaka while taking a Gram of us.

'You're in my Insta Story now and that's as real as it gets,' This was all the validation I needed for our fair-weather friendship.

'Hope we meet again slash take care slash good luck,' I captured what we were both thinking I feel because we both smiled.

'Hanky Panky pass the bong,' a woman's voice insisted from afar. He was being summoned by a woman only known as "Mermaid". I wouldn't miss the trance on till 6am most nights while people partied and ate food that didn't belong to them which resided in the communal fridge.

'Hey Hank, you have any chewy or something?'

'NO,' he laughed and headed back toward to the couch of people.

When I went back to my room my one-night stand was fully clothed and tying up his laces on the end of the bed. I remembered, how he stuck his head under my shirt the night before to reach me for a kiss and make fun of its oversized style.

'Steal heaps?' I asked as he adjusted his hair in the mirror. The night before, he'd told me he wasn't over his ex who cheated on him. I was already undoing my pants as I said, 'Aren't we all trying to forget someone?'

I grabbed my backpack. The lift was still broken. Someone had gotten stuck in there for hours last week; they were the guinea pig punished for attempting to use it. I heard the opening harmonies for "Silver Soul" begin as we descended the stairs. The poetry was cutting through the keyholes of the doors I closed behind us. I imagined it was lost on them in that smokey room like most things were I guess. He tried to reach out to hold my hand a couple of times as I mimed "It's happening again." I had paid a month's rent as a fail-safe, in case this was another dream left unfulfilled. I didn't want to come back; it would mean I had failed in moving on. That was the crux of it. Sometimes decisions are formed purely from trying to set the wheels in motion for things other than what you don't want to do.

'Have a good weekend with your sister.'

'You mean brother?' he said with nonchalance as he adjusted his crotch through his tight jeans. I nodded. He kissed my dry mouth. I'd decided to brush with a bottle of water in the car later to just get on the road. I was badly prepared for the short kiss goodbye.

'I'll text.' We didn't exchange numbers and I watched him stroll down the street and back into the wild where he came from where he'd be a more crucial figure in someone else's story.

As we drove out I noticed the brunchers were out in all their glory, sitting alfresco, taking pictures of their eggs bennie. As we passed them Babe yelled out 'See you later motherfuckers' and let out a maniacal laugh. She yelled it further down the street to the masseuse girls smoking in their robes on the street relaxing after a busy night of flattery and lube, no doubt. 'See you later motherfuckers!' She yelled it into a street filled with weekend warriors, their illustrated shock made us burst out laughing.

I decided I felt so liberated I'd flash my sports bra to a couple wearing matching polo's on our way out. Babe followed suit, except she was bra-less.

'Babe!' We gave out a hearty cackle while Teddy ignored us awkwardly and focussed on the road.

It felt good leaving the city. Maybe I'd miss the blue-water, the blue collars, the white paper sails on the harbour and the white collars beating their desires into the pavement nine to five. The beauty of this city was always protected by affluence, and it meant that this place was always foaming with energy because people needed to hustle in order to possess a slice of it; it was always demanding pace. Though in between blithe there was apathy, and so much loneliness.

We were leaving this madness behind, leaving behind the sirens that wailed through the shutters at night, the local street alcoholics fighting over where to drink next or where to sleep, the rats shrieking in the alleys hungry again, the occasional pointless firework, the couple next door fucking. Someone was always getting fucked in this city: winning or losing, fucking or getting fucked; I couldn't discern the difference anymore, nor could anyone else I think. We could ignore it with new kinds of highs, old bedroom nuptials and fairy light confessions with the shared creed of 'you got screwed too huh?' But it was all temporary relief. This small world you made with the curve of a blade, gently, with persistence and a tense hand. This world where you placed faces wandering amongst its columns, holy and fragile as sacrament. This world was not enough. The city and all its troubles were still waiting for you outside your diorama of being, your synecdoche of experience. The only way to feel safe in this world now was to pursue the version you wanted before you were afraid. That's what I had been deciding slowly for the last few years. I was getting ready to get out!

As we moved further out of the city, the roads began to widen and I began to breathe deeper. The buildings became shorter and sparser; the open road came shortly after. The open road makes you feel like you're in a state of chasing something cursory and leaving something permanent. I reclined in the back. Babe and Teddy's voices became muffled as I let myself feel heavy against the car seat. I was falling asleep. I was finally resting.

I had a disturbing sense that someone was watching me. That was what woke me up. When I opened my eyes Babe was licking her servo ice cream, she was right in my face and it made her break into a big smile knowing she had disturbed me without out a sound.

'What the fuck, Babe? Hate it when you do that!'

'We stopped to get supplies.'

'How long have we been driving for?' I wiped drool from the corners of my mouth.

'A couple of hours. We missed The Gong.'

'We missed The Gong? Shit. You could've woken me.'

'Teddy and I decided to stay on the highway. It's faster.'

Wollongong was my uni town. I got accepted into a writing course and Babe followed me down. We had a lot of good memories there, maybe too many to talk about. When I remembered them, or tried to talk about that part of my life, it felt like my rib cage closed up a bit. I knew living that life was forever gone and I needed to fight to keep them lucid.

I can say I loved the alchemy of surf culture and the pulsating steelworks that loomed in the background. I couldn't help but inject Fitzgerald's North Egg into it when I moved there. There were always parties on where musicians ended up jamming off-duty. Thirroul was home. The town was pretty and effortless like a salt breeze picking up an empty hammock. There was a group of eccentric lecturers who would often mishandle your literary insecurities with a shoulder shrug or a pause and rarely an agreement that your work was more deserving than a pass. The poet Wearne, in his mad rants, would leave you clues on how to be a better writer. Shady allowed her students to hypothetically place a gun to her head and force her to choose between character and plot, mid-lecture. Lectures spiralled into discussions; discussions moved into chats, chats oscillated between arguments and disagreements over eight dollar beer jugs and falling asleep on campus benches from drinking and talking. No one talked as much as we did and perhaps it was the last of the great conversations some of us would have.

It was the only time I felt electric as though I was plugged into something. People use the word 'community', but sometimes it felt like it was more absolute than that. Sometimes we'd go for nudie swims at the beach or Austinmer pools at dusk. We were present in the vastness of that blue; you could easily be a part of a synchronised routine through the blackness of the universe, or a fleck of gold glistening in the sunset, like amber adorning the finger of God. We were no longer random players in some sort of seasonal show. For a moment we were purposeful, deliberate and we coalesced.

Babe was always scared of the water but she was always there, waiting, laughing at our jiggly body parts, waiting with a towel in her hand.

We got out of the car at a town called Berry to get coffee and donuts. Berry was lush with the highway thinning out to two lanes. It was always busy on the weekends, designed for middle-class families who liked expensive wine and cheese, and whose time-to-money ratio allowed them to look for antiques in the country.

'The smell of coffee is the best smell!' Babe announced as some kids ran past us, much to her clear annoyance. 'Stupid kids.'

Teddy brushed my hand by accident as we walked, we ignored it but I was left thinking about his touch. I noticed it when he rested his elbow on my shoulder, as we waited for our order of donuts and coffee. I stood still barely speaking and enjoying him being close. The queue for the small silver food truck which sold the famous cinnamon sugar donuts began to snake around the corner. The people seemed to be all passing through. They had families in tow, children who were chocolate-faced, hyper, and already in their trunks and bathers anticipating their encounter with the season's last swim.

As we walked back with our food I yelled, 'So who's on dinner duty later?' Hoping it wouldn't be me.

'I'm happy to be sous chef.' Babe smelt a frangipani she'd collected off the ground which looked pretty but slightly trampled. She was a few steps ahead of us and she had to yell out to make her voice travel.

'I reckon we should pick up some fresh fish and prawns from Burrill Lake and BBQ those suckers,' I yelled ahead to Babe. There was a collective and excited 'Yeah!'

I used to fish with my Father around these parts. We sat in silence, listening to the birds, not talking, barely moving. I learned about ritual here with him and the meditative state of killing time. After he descaled the fish, he'd take it out to the beach and wash it in the smaller breaks. It was his tradition to bless it and send it into the afterlife with a final sense of home.'

He washed the unblinking fish in green crashing water and I watched the rainbow scales circling the white wash and gently being lulled into the next. I wanted to relive it with him, with Teddy. Maybe because I craved a sense of custom and the potency of being calm with another was now lacking in my life.

'Maybe we can go for a fish tomorrow morning?' I said hopeful.

'Yeah, sounds good. I'll let Babe know,' Teddy was in good spirits.

'She's a little bit scared of water and when I say little I mean she stays away from it. She doesn't even like having baths.'

Teddy grinned and gave me eyes as though he was saying, *Are you for real?*

'Yep, I know. She thinks it's because she drowned in a past life and she's still grieving.' I felt guilt tapping me on the shoulder, like we were leaving her out.

'Oh, we'll figure something out,' he winked.

I was aware of Babe. She eclipsed my movements even from afar and I felt her glances capture looks and interactions between Teddy and I. I felt she knew my intentions so I decided to sit with her in the front and blast the next couple of songs I knew she'd like.

When we were in view of the car I yelled, 'Shotgun!' It had taken us a while to find parking so we ended up parking in the middle of Berry.

I slept again till Nowra, the centre to a couple of satellite suburbs along the South Coast. It wasn't the prettiest. The bridge looked as though it went over the river of Lethe. The red brick buildings were tagged with graffiti and the park land usually contained a cricket pitch and few trees. The people appeared to be fine existing with the hand they'd been dealt; which was sometimes a hand-out from the government. This payment afforded them a couple beers, a couple of school shoes for growing feet, and the odd slap of the pokies on the weekend.

I left Babe in the car to find a bathroom and ran into Teddy. He was coming out of a sex shop. I pretended to not notice him until he was closer. He didn't think I'd seen him. It felt intrusive to ask what the fuck he was doing.

'Hey, snoring beauty.'

I almost asked him what he was doing in a sex shop, instead I asked, 'Where's the loo?' and he pointed to a sign that clearly said 'Toilets'.

'We're leaving in five. Babe and I got some stuff for the house.'

He came in close and whispered in my ear, 'I... wanted to let you sleep after all those donuts you ate, shhh.' He stayed close to me and let his eyes drift down to my mouth. I could feel his breath on my face, his finger slowly made its way to my lips. 'You've got sugar on your face nerd.' I felt the sandpapery scrape of the sugar between my lips and his index. We both laughed, though mine was more out of embarrassment.

Our plan was to just drive a couple more hours to a place called Lake Tabourie. There was a local grocer and a couple of other shops there and Teddy probably wanted us to smash out the rest of the trip and settle at the house. We were going to be there for two nights. Then we were meant to be making our way through to settle at our future snow-encrusted house.

'What's your favourite smell?' Babe squinted then touched Teddy's shoulders quickly between keeping her eyes on the road and sucking on her cigarette. I knew she was relaxed. Babe only asks unnecessary questions when she's no longer in survival mode. In everyday life her questions seemed more like accusations. In this instance, this was the best 'getting to know you' question. It was a step up from the 'how's this weather?' shit we performed with people on the daily.

'Let me think for a sec,' I said watching the pampas grass move in the coastal wind as we passed a field of them. I knew we were approaching a house on the hill. A boy I still loved told me about the Boab trees outside it. They had been transplanted from Africa and monitored for years in order for them to grow on a coastal cliff in Australia. They were so striking, these desert trees, surrounded by nothing but water and lush hills.

'It's definitely a toss-up.' Declared Teddy, determined with an answer he needed to get out. 'It's a toss-up between the smell of my own farts and...' before he could finish laughter broke out. We were expecting something insightful, as is the usual response. He kept his cool and waited for us to quieten down. 'And the smell of eggs and bacon cooking in the morning.' We both nodded, smiling, only just recuperating from the truism delivered on flatulence.

'Guess one follows the other,' said Babe, working out his answer, which made us all laugh again.

'Well,' Babe said, 'I love the smell of blown out birthday candles; I haven't smelled that in a couple years actually.' Silence coated us and we were all heavy in thought. Silence has the unique and strange ability to warp time as though it were plastic under a flame, or a candle melting under a birthday song.

The answer suddenly appeared and I said, 'Chlorine.'

It seemed to please both of them. I hoped they were imagining a clear blue pool, underwater tea-parties, and droplets drying on sun-kissed skin. I wondered if there was a smell I was yet to find which would make me feel more alive than the smell of chlorine. Maybe it was the smell of coffee brewing in the morning and a condensing window covered with snow. Maybe it was the crisp smell of mountain air, maybe that was the smell of Jindabyne or beyond.

'Smell is a good question,' Babe announced. I looked over at Teddy and noticed he was scrolling through his feed on Facebook.

'I deleted my Facie. I think it's like micro-plastic, it's just a big black hole of fear. We don't know what they're doing with our information or how this will all effect us down the track. Anyways it's fucked up.'

Babe was nodding while listening to my rant. 'For sure, I got rid of mine too,' she said while applying lip balm at a red light.

'Really?' Teddy was particularly struck by Babe's confession.

'Yeah, I have enough shit in my life I consume which is bad for me and I can't chemically avoid, and well Facebook and social media in general is now off that list. I missed the hits of dopamine at first from people double tapping but then... you know, you live. Now I just need to get into that mindset for everything.' I was laying on the backseat again and watching the clouds speed past the passenger window.

'Babe weed is good for you though. Smoking weed is like wearing a condom around your soul, whereas Facebook is evil,' I said as I took a strand of hair out of my mouth. 'It's legal in plenty of other countries which are far more progressive. Countries which aren't all about that dichotomy of criminal and puritan.' Teddy was listening intently.

'Hey one of my great, great, great grandfathers was one of those criminals,' Teddy said smiling with his palm floating in the air proudly. This country was fixated on worshipping criminals the right shade of pink.

'The best ones were,' I raised my own palms in mock animation.

'Fuck I love this song! Air is a good choice... is this the "QLD playlist?"'

'Yep,' I closed my eyes and nodded while singing the only English part of the song - 'Sexy Boy'; I heard Babe's voice join mine.

'Teddy, this is the playlist we made up that summer we went to Queensland for Aruna's wedding.'

'Best trip! Put all that good shit up our noses, made a hundred friends, danced till morning, beach and dive bars all day!'

The windows were all open and it felt like we were in the eye of the storm and we were riding it together. Youth is a powerful thing to feel pulsating through your decisions. That feeling felt like it'll be okay because you have time.

'I'm in charge of tonight's music,' Teddy made a point of saying.

My eyes suddenly saw an animal on the road.

'Babe watch out!' It was too late. I felt the initial impact of its body, the bones crushing under speed. Babe stopped the car.

'THE FUCK DID I JUST HIT?' Babe's hands were waving in the air, her eyes were afraid.

Teddy was asking her to calm down.

'I hit something!' She looked pale.

'I don't know.'

I stopped the music. She turned the engine off. We were quiet, just listening to the wind whip past.

'I can't just leave it there,' Teddy finally said. He got out of the car and I watched in the rear view mirror as he cautiously walked over to the animal. He took his jacket off and placed it over the body. He looked back at the car and I caught the expression on his face for a moment. He was upset. Babe kept her face on my shoulder. Teddy dragged what was left to the side of the road and walked back with more pace.

'Wren can you drive?' I nodded and moved to get in the driver's seat.

'Should we go to a hospital in case she's in shock? Is that a thing?'

'I'm fine,' she muttered the words after blowing her nose. 'I'm just upset, I'm not in shock. I feel fine.' Teddy and I looked at each other as he escorted her to the back.

'Ok, but we'll watch you and see if you're ok in the next while.'

I was driving slow and steady. The heavy pastures were contracting against my thoughts underneath. Above was a subtle peppering of cattle, still, and yet moving their chewing gullets.

'Wren, what did I hit?'

'It's okay Babe, it was an accident. Whatever it was, it didn't suffer.'

I drove into a local petrol station to get water and maybe run a hose on the car.

'I'll do that,' Teddy grabbed the bucket off me as I approached the car, 'You go get us a couple bottles of water and something to eat.'

Babe was in the car laying on the back seat resting and gently sobbing. I could see Teddy through the store window with his yellow gloves, throwing some sort of slop into a bucket and wringing the dirty sponge. His face was screwed up with disgust. As I approached the car again I could hear him saying to himself, 'This is fucked up.'

He dumped the contents of the bucket into the gutter. I saw the water rush through the iron grill, separating the bits of carcass from the soapy liquid. The animal was just an abstract of wet fur and pink now, purging into more filthy water like some sort of reverse distillery of death. I thought, *is this what's to come for all of us eventually? Matter and inconvenience?* What a way to go, being part of some polluted collective rushing under the streets, under the yawns of paperbark trees and people spent. Will these gutters fulfil their design and hide this death from the pulse of the world above. Would our bodies too, angular bone and tattered meat, be expected to just join the waters of Lethe and be commanded to forget a life lived? After the pomp of a black party, would we also be sanctimoniously tossed into a ditch or a furnace, to be spat out into the wilderness of the afterlife. I suppose that is what some people may call 'grace', to return to something bigger. All I knew is that we were in the middle of nowhere, with the ocean crashing somewhere in the next few k's. It seemed strange that life could end so abruptly, so close to paradise or maybe so far.

I got into the backseat with Babe and passed her a chocolate bar and water. She sat up and drank. It seemed to calm her. She looked at me.

'My mum always told me our cat Mimi had ran away. Years later she told me she found it dead in the front yard. She said she felt bad, it looked like she died in pain, all curled up like that. Part of me wishes I knew that back then and part of me wishes I didn't know it now.' There it was, no grand declarations of loss. Though Babe's story was austere in plot, it was a pin dropped on how we are all governed by this randomness, this finality; death is always in the details.

I decided to stay with Babe in the back to make sure she was okay.

We drove mostly in silence afterwards. Teddy caught me looking at him while he drove. His eyes locked with mine in the rear-view. Babe was asleep.

'What are you really running from Wren?' The rear-view mirror showed his eyes were full of expression though I couldn't see his mouth.

'I don't know,' I lied.

'Liar,' he said without hesitation. It reminded me of the way we have those conversations in private just with ourselves, but we're rehearsing it to happen with someone else. He seemed almost disappointed with my answer, like the answer I said in his imaginary rehearsal was way more glamorous or interesting. He looked back to the road, now slightly illuminated by that light that only dusk can create, slight and mournful like a cooling sun.

'What do you think I'm running from?' He looked out to the road lined with boney banksias blackened from Summer's backburning.

'I think you're running from answers. If you stayed in the city longer you'd get an answer to your future that you wouldn't like.'

'Nope, I don't think so.' He was bluffing to get something out of me. It was something I'd practiced when I wanted to dissect someone. If you bluff someone with faux insights they either correct you because they don't want to be misunderstood, or they concede. Misrepresentation usually wins out because we all want to have some command on what people think about us.

'You only know that, Teddy, because it's your reason. You're projecting your shit here.'

'Well no. I'm not running from solutions I don't agree with,' he said, 'I'm running from problems I created to be honest. Yes, yes I know that those always catch up. I'm just trying to enjoy bought time.'

'Fuck, that's bleak Teddy.'

I wanted to ask more but I knew I'd have to disclose my own stuff and I wasn't ready, maybe I didn't know how to open up, so I let silence fall till it was OK to unroll my manuscript and scribble under the light of my phone. Babe was snoring next to me and we were all alone in our worlds for now.

Babe woke up, she looked oddly rested, although tears have a type of endorphin in them which is designed to calm your body and sedate it. This is likely why you always feel tired after you cry.

'It was a cat wasn't it?'

I didn't want to upset her again so I didn't answer.

'I saw its face before the car hit it. I killed somebody's pet. Someone is going to be looking for it, worried, hoping it'll come back.'

She began to cry again. Babe had never killed anything; unlike me. She seemed so small in that moment. I fixed her hair up and put my arms around her, and said, 'They'll get a new cat, Babe, probably a younger and cuter one.' This didn't stop her from crying; shockingly enough my bad joke didn't hit the mark. She always knew what to say.

When we arrived at the house, we walked through and sussed out our digs for the next couple of days. There were two rooms. Babe and I would share the master and Teddy had the single. The house was all shells and nautical themes in the bathroom, and brown carpet throughout, except the linoleum kitchen. There were no pictures of people just potpourri baskets and a cheap print of a naked couple and swan. We wanted to enjoy the last of summer before heading inland to Jindabyne, and this was homely and cheap.

Unpacking the car, I noticed most of the homes around us had no cars in the drive-way; they weren't big decadent homes, just places you may have visited the odd time in your school holidays. The BBQ was clean, luckily, so Teddy started cooking some sausages.

He took a sip of his beer. 'I like this place.' He winked at me.

'So how does Maddie feel about you coming with us?'

He took a sip of his beer. 'She's okay with it, I think. We don't really talk much right now.'

'What? Why?' he was so matter of fact about it, not emotionless but definitely removed. He nodded to himself as he sipped his beer again. Avoiding my eyes altogether. 'Do you miss her?' He took another sip instead of answering immediately.

'Yes. It's part of the reason why I needed to get away. It's over.'
Those words were so definitive.

'How do you know when it's over?' I wanted to know when people stopped trying when a child is involved. For whatever reason now, Teddy was making himself known to me. I wanted to dissect the roles he was appointed as a man; I wanted to understand its own explicit pain. Teddy was father, husband, confidant and friend, and the pain he felt to each of those things made him real. His hurt made him real because it meant that those titles weren't just titles they were his life and his distinct failures.

'It just is,' was the only explanation he gave.

'Does Agi know?' It was a bit of a dumb question because she was so young; she wouldn't understand why she didn't see her parents together anymore. She'd just sense the disconnect. Her life would liken to the gentle pulling of a thread on a jumper, unravelling to her new life of schedules and weekends at her Dad's place.

'I see a happy little girl but I don't see her all the time. I miss her at night and putting her to bed. That used to be her time to tell me things, just little things she saw that day or tell me she loved me. All I can say is that she knows I'm not there now, the why part is probably too big for her to understand.'

'Who will Agi stay with?'

'With Maddie, of course. It makes sense. Agi will always come first.' He added too much salt on some fish he was marinating as he spoke.

'As far as Madeleine and I go, we're over. We didn't look after each other through the years.' That phrase was recycled; I'd heard married, middle class people use it when they lost control of their spouse or themselves. Control is like light, people only realise it's lacking, when they're sitting in the dark.

'We thought being wildly in love would make us different, then when we realised it didn't. We hoped family life would bond us back together, but over the years we hurt each other pretty fucking bad.' He polished his beer off. 'Did I see us here, when we decided to get married? No. Did I imagine days I couldn't see Agi because it wasn't my turn? No. Did I imagine waking up alone again in an apartment with just my things? No. I could say life is shitty sometimes, but that's what people say who don't know where they went wrong.'

He was trying to turn down the heat on the BBQ. He was burning most of the sausages on the hot plate and stuck some fish fillets on for good measure.

'I would've stayed unhappy too. It's all I know, it's all I've been taught. I didn't want to teach that to Agi...'

The smell of burning meat was being mixed with the smell of salt from the ocean, it reminded me of how much I liked being outside. The breeze lifted a small pile of serviettes I'd placed mid-table, along with the chilling wine bottles bathing in a salad bowl of ice. Babe was inside cutting up veggies. There was an odd sense of domestic harmony between us. I sensed this was part of the reason why he had been so candid and open about everything. I wanted to know him again.

'Does Madeleine still love you?' I tried to pose the question as a friend not someone who was interested in him as anything more. The real question I wanted to ask was, did he still love her? But I dared not ask that because I was scared he would say yes.

He took a chunk out of the fish and put it in his mouth, fanning the heat away with his hand.

'I think she does. Family is the only place you feel like you could maybe have a sense of belonging, even when you're not wanted.'

I nodded but I disagreed and decided to make my position clear.

'My father was like a phantom limb. I stopped calling him dad. It went from dad to father and then father to just his first name, then to nothing because he was a stranger. I was unrolling my school skirt and waiting for the bus at the shopping centre , when I saw him. He asked me how my mother was doing. Eventually I said fine. I told him I forgave him. He asked what for? I said I didn't know entirely, but maybe one day I'd mean it. I was 13. That was the last time I ever spoke to him. So I don't know if I agree with you about belonging even when you're not wanted.'

'Your Father was an asshole Wren, different thing altogether.' I was stuck remembering him, talking about that mess felt good.

'He'd tell my mum and I no one loved us but him. We were nothing without him. I believed him, till he died. I think I locked that away till now.' He turned the BBQ off and had his full attention on me; it made me uneasy I was using him as catharsis.

He shook his head and gave me a big hug, the type which envelopes you, the type when a man wraps his arms around your shoulders but somehow ends up covering your ears too.

'It's important, being a father.' I said, muffled by his embrace and I felt his head nod in agreement.

Babe came outside with a second salad bowl but full of salad. 'I think I should throw some cards after dinner or maybe, I don't know, I just need to do something. Have you ever had your fortune told?'

'No.' Teddy's tone was soft and cautious. Babe wiped snot with her sleeve.

'I just need something to get my mind off things.'

'Sounds good,' I said, putting my arms around Babe's waist.

We were starving, we ate quickly, barely stopping, we picked the salad out of the bowl with our fingers. We drank wine in mismatched glasses. Teddy filled my glass up with red when it still had white in it. The deck of Tarot cards was perfectly stacked, untouched. We were digesting before we started stacking the plates and headed inside to settle on the couches.

Teddy put his playlist on and grabbed a brown paper bag out of his satchel. We were heading for drunk.

The opening chords of Marvin Gaye's "Heard It Through the Grapevine" started.

'Love this song,' Babe announced. She started dancing with Teddy by awkwardly spinning him, her outreached arm causing him to bend his body awkwardly and making me laugh.

'I never know which version I prefer but I think it's this one for now,' he smiled and took a huge sniff out of a popper. 'Got this for nostalgia sake.' His face relaxed into a toxin-infused Cheshire cat grin.

'That's what you were buying from the sex shop!' I pointed, relieved.

'I thought you were buying porn or sex cuffs!' Babe snatched the small glass bottle from him and shoved it up her nostril and languidly slid into the couch. I piled next to her to have a smell. Amyl was used as a muscle relaxant for anal but it was also used to fry your brain. It was a short, sharp type of high which mostly felt like a giddy headache. It was best sniffed via the open mouth of the glass bottle. Though I had seen people dip cigarettes in it and inhale it that way. The bottle was enough for me. The chemicals whirred through each capillary on my face. I imagined my brain was warming up slowly through movement again, like fingers stretching out before they pounded the keys of a freshly-tuned piano. My mind was frenetic, alive, readying itself for a journey, like a locust upturning its sub-continental wings for travel. Once you were ready all that was left was to surrender to the surrealism the substances allowed you to feel connected to. You're the curve in a climatic moan, the white mush spilling out of a dreaming roach on the floor, the bearded man sleeping outside your locked door, asking for you to open before his thirst for blood had lead him away again. You're the rotting leaves in the rain gutters of your childhood home, the egg cooking on the driveway on a forty degree day, the sugar cube melting under a stream of boiling water, the sip of that sweet tea after. Your fingers burying themselves in a nest of hair, and all the while falling inside of it all, you heard music as new voices and the instruments were conversing, you hoped you'd never be just old you again. Somehow you'd found the combination no one else knew which could make you feel boundless, at least for a while. To surrender, which such few knew how to do. To be capable of transcending a lifetime of building disciplinary habits, constructs of yourself, expectations and hope. This was all just 21st Century alchemy. If we were to be seperated from each other we would perish as does the fruit from the root. Together, we could defy this. We turned each other from stone to skin; powder to bones; lead to gold. We transmuted sex to adoration, and adoration to purpose, like blow flies searching for shit to call home. We were proving that the life we thought not possible was, just somewhere else. We were finally free to love the other.

'What am I, 150 years old? Nobody buys porn anymore. It's called streaming.' We both shot him looks. Babe lit a cigarette and pulled me onto the couch to dance on the furniture. Teddy was fiddling with his Spotify account.

'I like the grit in John Fogerty's voice, personally,' I said.

'But the soul in Marvin's version,' he pleaded. He warmed up a plate while Babe and I danced to "Everyday People". Then he popped two pink pills inside a folded 20 dollar note. He got out his wallet and picked a credit card and began to crush the two pills inside the folded note, then, like an artisan, he smoothed it out until there was just powder inside. MD was cheaper than blow. He lined up a row on the plate. I noticed a picture of Maddie and Agi in the clear plastic part of his wallet; only throw back or expensive wallets still have that spot for pictures. Teddy's was the former. I remembered a wallet like that one glistening new in his room all those years ago, sat upon torn Christmas paper. He held the plate up to Babe and smiled while she snorted it.

'Fuck Teddy, can you make these any fatter?'

I took my line. I vacuumed the piercing pink powder with velocity and settled at the basecamp of my mind. It eased into my body, which was accustomed to feeling reality clanging like a Marinetti poem. The pupils grasped for light and relinquished it, an open orifice feeding on shadows cut by the smooth yellow lamplight.

'Should we go out?' Teddy suggested. But I already knew the feeling of shuffling sticky money at bars, filling your mouth up with someone else's breath, filling your bed with kinetic naked bodies.

'Not tonight,' I said. Teddy sat back down and started to line up the next one. Babe took his wallet and inspected the picture in it. I snorted another candy-pink line and felt it hit me almost immediately.

'Fuck! Maddie. Is. So. Pretty.' Babe smiled a lazy closed mouth smile, 'But want to know what? I think you're prettier than her!' She looked at him dead in the eye and took a drag of her cigarette. The fluorescent powder released itself from my nasal cavity into my bloodstream, breaking away like brittle bricks. Everything started to accelerate again.

'Fuck off, I ain't pretty,' Teddy scoffed.

'No? Well I think we can make you look pretty. At least just for tonight maybe. With some eyeliner?' I suggested. Babe held her hands with palms placed together pensively. Decorating Teddy's face with outrageous, whorish makeup while in this high was a great idea.

'Please?' Babe chimed in. 'PULEEEEASSSSEE?'

He took a whiff of the popper and giggled the word, 'Fine'. He was so high he didn't care. 'It can be an ode to my

Goth days,' he said matter-of-factly. Babe and I made our way to the bathroom. Selecting the right tools to make him beautiful would be vital.

'Do you think he wants a threesome?' Babe sniffed while I was fishing for my untouched Miss Moss blue eyeshadow in my makeup bag.

'I fucking hope not.' I didn't think of her like that at all so I wanted to shut it down, but then maybe I didn't want to rule it out.

'What? It might be fun,' she grinned. 'He can just fuck both of us. We don't have to do stuff with each other, unless you want to.' She cupped my breasts jokingly and sniffed hard again.

I was turned on by the idea of Teddy. I wanted to know how hairy his chest was. Was he rough in bed? Was he gentle? Did he like his asshole being licked? Did he like dirty talk? What sound did he make as he came? Was he sweet after the fact?

'No way, Babe. Besides, you've already screwed him,' I laughed.

'Anyways, I don't remember that. Two reasons: we were wasted, and it was years ago. Besides, I think he's got a bit of experience behind him now, he'll be much better.' She was putting lip gloss on her small elfin like lips.

'No, he's going through shit. He's getting divorced.'

'Even more reason to fuck him back to single life!' We both burst out laughing. Then we both shushed each other's laughter, hoping he hadn't heard that exchange. We both fell into our own worlds. I was applying a thick line of eyeliner to my eyes as Babe sung the same Frank lyrics over and over to herself in a sickly sweet falsetto.

When we got back to the living room, Teddy was lighting some candles in the sitting room. This garnered a hard elbow from Babe intended to be a 'told you he's trying to get us into bed' gesture.

I started to try and tie his hair up in a Shih Tzu pony tail at the front, while Babe put eyeliner on the top of his eyelids, wing style.

'Teddy, for fucks sake you're looking a better woman than both of us,' Babe joked.

Teddy was midway through rolling a cigarette and letting us do what we wanted to his face when the Grizzly Bear song "Three Rings" came on. Babe jumped up and headed to the plate to rack herself another line.

'I love this song.' It probably reminded her of that steam punker who ghosted her. She'd tried to date him but really he was already dating himself. We nicknamed him Nick the Dick.

'Babe don't mess with the playlist please. Each song is strategically placed to create overall balance, a symetry if you will.' He closed his eyes and said, 'This song is like a secret that keeps hiding itself from you after you think you've found it.'

Teddy seemed genuinely happy in that moment. We started to peel away into our own levels of high. Babe was in self-adventure mode and disappeared, as she often did. I always internalised the highs and liked to be still with just the right amount of moving to the music. This time it was different, I was free from myself and staring at Teddy. Teddy gestured if I wanted a rollie. I mimed yes, not able to do much more. He was singing the lyrics to me, watching me with his heavily lined eyes.

I wanna show you my bad side
I wanna be the guy who's right

There was the exact amount of reluctance in his voice, to make it charming. I watched the tip of his tongue run along the paper's edge. He gently rolled it. He started rolling a second one with the same delicate method. He looked through me as he licked the paper and sang both to himself and me:

Don't you be so reasoned
Don't you know that I can make it better
Don't you ever leave me

Don't you feel it all come together

The music came back in and he lit the cigarette he'd rolled and passed it over to me.

For the remainder of the song I couldn't stop smiling. I imagined what the story of our seduction would sound like at parties when people asked how we ended hooking up. Would this be our song? Teddy coming back into my life felt like it was maybe a second chance but we would have to be careful. I signalled I was getting another drink; I needed some cold air in my lungs.

Teddy always chose someone else - Babe, Maddie - after disappearing, he was here again. Was I his last choice or his first? I suddenly wanted to be the family in his wallet. You never stop loving the people you love; it all just shifts its intensity to the next person but you never forget. Love is a series of stories you always remember, a series of movements ruminating in the unconscious, like lashes closing to sleep, or your skin reacting to the cold. Love exists like a limb moving to music, it was proof that someone else was there for a while. Or maybe, you were capable of being someone else. I wanted to know the truth about why Teddy disappeared but maybe truth was the more mundane side of it, truth is the administrator of reality. Love owes it's potency to transcending truth anyway and all that is left quivering after is bare experience. Why he disappeared, I suppose didn't matter so much, what mattered now was that he had come back for a little while.

I could hear the hard bodies of the moths colliding with the open light bulb of the patio. I read that moths use the moon as an indicator for their flight path, a sort of compass. It was how they understood what was up and what was down. Man-made light sources fucked with their sense of direction. We had doomed them to covet the wrong light. Because of us they were always lost and died prematurely. Didn't they know they were doomed? Good things didn't happen to stupid animals, no matter how small they were in the scheme of things. I licked the note I had taken my lines with. I checked for excess powder and I unrolled it and felt the waxen paper between my thumb and finger. I Googled money once, just to see. The top two things people searched for were 'what was it?' and 'can I get it free?'. We all want something for nothing. To prove it we invented paper. Paper we turned to polymer. This plastic we exchange for our bodies, for our ethics. Plastic which governs our levels of kindness to each other and dictates our presence. Plastic we invented just so we can deplete and erase where we see fit. Plastic we use to strip each other down to our colours and creeds. Plastic which allowed the corrupt to walk free to do as they please, to rape every cunt that asked for it, every cunt that dressed to get it, every cunt that just didn't say no enough, or clearer, or louder. Colourful plastic we used to destroy each other to the sound of the last nail being hammered through the earth's last good vein. Why should I not destroy this evil before it destroys me? Would I even flinch if I burned this?

I held the lighter up to the fifty-dollar bill as steadily as I could, for as long as I could, partly to disprove the myth of the moth and the flame. I watched the yellow plastic slowly curl in the heat and finally placed it on the concrete kneeling over it, feeding it more fire but protecting it from the wind. It started to burn properly and I felt as though it had met its end in a more honest way rather than spending it and feeding it back into a system of tills breaking it down into smaller numbers, only to end up in strange and slimy hands with the stink of want. I'd desecrated it as though it was just matter, because it was. I smiled as I watched the black smoke undress it to its true form. I stood there watching it, till I trampled the flame and kicked it away into the dark before lighting my cigarette. One less thing to worship, one less thing to miss.

I heard the glass door sliding open, and at first I hoped it was Teddy, and then I craved the simplicity of my friendship with Babe instead of him. I felt lips placed gently on my neck. I could smell him; he was tree and earth. He was heat. My instinct was to move away from it.

'What?' He smiled, slightly embarrassed.

'You caught me by surprise is all.'

'Always pulling away, Wren, always.' This was said in jest but I knew he was being passive aggressive because I had moved away. Was he blaming me for this unspoken tension between us? We never touched like this before or gotten this close.

'You can't fake intimacy Teddy,' I felt aware that maybe we were rushing past something important, something we were missing which didn't match up. His head was nodding with me. 'You can't.'

The silence appeared to agitate him, well that and my reaction to his affection which looked unreturned. The rain was hitting so hard it was was activating the motion sensor and turning the flood lights on.

'What's that type of character called again?' He had positioned himself to be face to face with me. I was confused. 'You told me about it the morning after Babe and I slept with each other.'

'I don't know, I talk a lot of shit. That was years ago.' I lied.

'This wasn't shit, Wren, it was true. It was the biggest truth you've managed. You said there are only two types of characters in books and in life. Passive ones that let shit happen to them, and active ones. The difference is when you read one you become infuriated by them. They don't change their life because they can; they change their life out of fear, or worse their life doesn't change because of their own ennui. I always wondered which one you thought I was. I kind of figured I was the latter but I guess by your definition you were always the passive character too.'

'Yeah, black says the kettle,' I smiled sarcastically with the corner of my mouth.

'I'm here now, aren't I?! I'm fucking trying, which is more than what you're doing. I want this, I came here for you Wren!'

'Well, you don't get to choose me now. What's done is done. You made your decision long ago and now this isn't, well this can't happen. Go home to your wife Teddy, what are you even doing here?'

'You know you talk about it like everything is done! Written! But you carry that fucking book of yours around, re-writing things all the time. Are you that sad you only hope to change fictional characters? You don't want to change anything else? You're hiding in your writing; you hide behind your failure to pursue it. Why?'

'Because Teddy, fictional characters don't fucking demand to be loved when they haven't earned it. I don't want you in my life now. You're wrong. I was active. I chose to not have you, I chose to not find you when you left town and then I chose to not have you as a friend when I found out you were married. The same way you chose to not have me in your life and now it's gone to shit and I don't really understand what you want from me.'

'Why are you so angry at me Wren? It's me, not your father.'

He used information I'd entrusted to sanction some sort of a point. I was hurt but I couldn't walk away. I wanted to shine a blinding light into his eyes and trick him like those moths.

'You knew how I felt about you Teddy. You fucking knew it!'

'That is so unfair, Wren. How could I possibly have known?' His rational question infuriated me. He was being coy.

'Are you performing your rationality because you imagined this confrontation before? Or are you defending yourself because it's muscle memory from your fucked up marriage?'

I sensed that I cut him, which I was pleased about, but also afraid. It needed to be done, we needed to pierce the boil to let it drain.

'I can't read angst-ridden, teenage girl minds! We were kids and fuck Wren! You were hard work, and you were all bones, eyes and anger, so much fucking anger.' His palms were open, and we were breathing heavily, exhausted from pulling deep into the past from our high. 'How could I know, Lawrence?'

'Because you loved me too!' I noticed his mascara was running. These words were an accusation bursting through the layers of our story. Like a cracked water pipe. The silence was punctuated by the moths colliding against the hot glass of the bulbs and the storm moving through wet tree branches.

'You fucked her,' I pointed inside through the closed door, to where I imagined Babe was probably snorting more pills or trying to shave a stuffed toy or writing a poem, or whatever it was Babe did when she was high. 'You fucked every pussy that came within your eye line and then you told me about them and how you thought you loved them, and in the end all those years ago, you chose my best friend over me. You fucked my only friend! Who, by the way, hated you and made fun of you behind your back!' I raised my arms in the air. 'She never gave two shits about you. She only had sex with you to rub it in my face because *she* knew how I felt. So why have you come back? You won!'

'I could never have you. So I took the closest thing to you all the time and I gave up eventually. I think that means you won.' All I could think about was the last couple of years and somehow everything seemed to be his fault.

'Fuck you.' Now I wasn't even thinking, I was just reacting to him. We were standing a few metres apart. He was standing by the edge of the patio, on the edge of the darkness, with the sound of the hostile ocean pushing hair over his face, the wind framing his silhouette.

We heard the door unlock and slide open, slowly on the rails.

Babe was standing there, her face was frozen in an expression I'd never seen before. We were all out here and aware of how deep that knife could go. Her eyes ignored Teddy, they were on me.

I was wiping my eyes with my fists gearing up to save face. She closed the door. We heard the engine start, and then she was gone.

I pictured her angrily screening each call I made. I was in such a state of panic for her safety, I failed to notice her phone had been left behind and was buzzing on the kitchen counter, in front of me.

Why did I give a shit about what happened between them all those years ago? I knew Babe was fucking emotionally stunted, I should have been more diplomatic.

'Do we call the police?' Teddy asked pacing on the kitchen linoleum.

'She has drugs in her system and so do we! I hope the police don't fucking find her, do you?' He didn't answer. 'Besides, we don't want her jailed, we just want her to be safe.'

'She's a danger to herself out there *and* to other people. She fucking killed a cat earlier when she was paying attention!' He had a point.

'Should we try and order a cab so we can go out and try finding my car.'

'We're at Lake Tabourie! Not Surry Hills, Teddy, cabs don't just roll up around here.'

'Well, we're going to have to wait it out.' He gave up offering pointless suggestions. 'She'll cool down and come back soon.'

The music was off, we were sitting on the couch quietly. He was on his phone and I was still high and tapping my fingers on the arm of the sofa. It was enough to let my mind wander. We both would react with hope when we saw a car headlight filter through the white living room curtains, and then be clearly disappointed when it wasn't her.

The high was wearing off or maybe it wasn't. I started to miss that place where everything I felt was fuzzier and less threatening, like a dog's teeth showing through a muzzle.

'I realised I loved you when you were the first person I told that Franz had taken his own life. I hadn't seen him since we were teenagers but I missed him like I'd just seen him yesterday. You were there for me and I loved you for it. And I always imagined that girl I loved to be out there still.' We were calm and just waiting for it all to unfold now. Teddy was looking at a part of the rug that had started to un-weave under the coffee table. He was touching it with his toe pensively.

'I always thought of you. Every time I ate fresh-cut tomatoes on toast, or sardines, which Maddie hated. I'd think of you when I'd listen to "English Summer Rain" on my way to work, or any Radiohead. I'd think of you when I smelt weed, or when I mismatched my socks. Even though I was with Maddie, somehow I always imagined that girl I loved to be out there still. She was out there strumming her guitar softly enough in the night for no-one to hear, but I could. She was smiling, fighting, sometimes both. And I wanted to be with her so bad. But she'd tell me no, not yet.'

He ran his fingers along his gums with the residue on the plate near him. He seemed to be distancing himself from his words that way.

'In my mind she'd say, "Go away, I'm not ready." And then I'd get impatient and want to pull her in again, but she wasn't looking for another complication.'

He was looking at me now, though he was somewhere else imagining her, this woman.

'Her joy, her charm; I wanted it to all to come to me, to make its way into my life. But she'd tell me to keep waiting because she was still not ready. And I would... wait and wait... for her to accept me. She makes no apologies because she was living her life, as purely as she could. I always thought when she's ready to let me in, when she's finally ready... then, then maybe I'll be permitted to love her forever.'

I let him finish and I watched him put his card into his wallet. He gestured to the picture in his wallet. 'It's not Maddie because I still imagined that girl to be out there, restless and thinking of me, maybe we'd find each other, maybe not. Sounds like bullshit doesn't it? But it's not.'

My mind couldn't move fast enough to understand the gravity of what he was saying so it felt unreal, at the time we were on our path to becoming who we are. All those late night conversations in our pyjamas, our hallway jokes, those nights we thought we figured something out till the sun came up and showed us our hubris. Those days where we used a tea bag twice and jumped the train station gates, those years with no direction stifled with too much freedom, those years were everything. We were both there and it fucking meant something, if not to anyone but to us. I never stopped loving Teddy, I'd never known someone the way I did him. I felt my eyes wander to the window for headlights. I wanted to fall into this world that had lapsed people and time but I felt angry still. I don't know why.

'That similar to the speech you made to Maddie when you married her?' I looked at his eyes and all at once I admitted to myself that I loved him still, even after all this time. I moved toward him.

He grabbed me, his breath was rushing through me before I could finish. Every hair on my body was leaning into him. We connected to each other immediately. My mind was completely alight, moving through the ebb and flow of a possible sexual encounter. The soft kissing which became biting, the sliding cotton against my pubis and the ghostly sticky, slick forming between my thighs, I was imagining feeling more of him.

Our kissing became more aggressive, and I sensed his hands wanted to touch other parts of my body. I wanted to beg him with instructions on how to touch me, how to move me but instead I pulled him onto the couch with me and positioned myself to be the small spoon.

'Teddy, let's not do this tonight, let's not fuck things up this soon. Not till we know Babe is okay.' I wanted us to have a long story. The last good one. But I didn't want it to start like this. We were high, Babe was missing, and his marital bed was barely cold. There would be another time we could be together which was guiltless and pure.

'I know,' he sighed, and moved a strand of hair from the nape of my neck and kissed it gently. I tried to concentrate on falling asleep.

I didn't turn to look at him once, like Orpheus, I just knew he was there. Through his calm and steady breathing of sleeping, I thought of our future. I imagined us smiling at each other with fuzzy teeth in our temporary bed while fireworks crackled on a Tulum street. I wanted to see the Amalfi Coast with him and lay on its burning sands with him by my side. I knew he'd make me laugh, and I'd see the world his way once in a while, we'd be good friends to each other. One day he'd let me down. But I was tired of being disappointed in people. I always left before the pendulum swung in my favour for happiness because I was afraid. I was tired of not knowing anyone, but more so I was tired of no-one knowing me. Morning started to stretch through the checkerboard of white sky and grey clouds. I kept hoping to hear the car pull up and I fell back asleep waiting.

I woke up hours later, disturbed by the afternoon light. I checked and saw that the car was parked crookedly. Teddy was still asleep. He sensed I was stirring and started to wake.

'She's home.' I whispered.

We got up and searched the house. The colder months were beginning to set in. The curtains on the patio were billowing in from the open glass door. She must've been down by the water. I saw her walking down by the beach and I wanted to throttle her for her stunt, and hug her simultaneously. I didn't know which one I'd do first.

'Babe!' As I approached her she was frowning and looked like she was welling up. 'I can't fucking believe you pulled that shit!' I yelled.

'Fuck you, bitch!' Her face distorted when she spat the words at me. 'Did you enjoy my sloppy seconds?' She screamed. Her rage stopped me immediately though it didn't stop her. She was storming over to me. 'I may fuck everyone but at least I didn't split up a family like you're doing with Maddie and his daughter. Fucking hypocrite, you're worse than me. You're the real deal, you're the slut fucking home-wrecker.'

'You absolutely annihilated Pete's marriage! After your pussy of death cursed both of them!' I laughed.

'You think you're so much better than me, Lawrence, you always have.'

'Babe, you destroy everything you touch and I'm the last one. Not even your sister wanted to be your sister anymore.' She started to laugh in a faux and haughty way which made her face look sinister.

'At least now I know you really are a psycho. You don't care about anyone but yourself. You're disgusting! That thing you flushed down the toilet has a better life now than it would have had with you. You would've been a shittier mother than you are a friend and trust me that's pretty shitty!'

She screamed the last word 'shit' in my face but I heard every curve of the letters in the words that made that sentence up. With that, I mustered all the strength I had and slapped her as hard as I could in her face. Her nose started bleeding; she looked shocked like someone who had never felt blood spilled from her peaceful, cold body. She touched the stream of blood, seemingly shocked by the odd sensation of its warmth on her hand. I didn't know this till now, I didn't know I could bring myself to this violence. It was in me but I had never seen it. I held the sleeve of my hoodie up to help with the bleeding.

'Don't touch me. You're fucking dead to me!' She screamed. She started running into the water. I let her.

She semi-swam out, though she was terrified of the big surf.

'I'm going to get her, surf's too big.' Teddy appeared. I watched him run out as I stood there with my bloody sleeve. Teddy dove head first into an oncoming set, and disappeared. I could see Babe in the distance. She was too scared to go further out and started to try head in, it was clear she could barely swim and she kept trying to lie on her back to backstroke and kept swallowing water. She hadn't gotten far but her face was made of pure fear as she doggy-paddled back and semi-recovered on a sand bank. The big surf during the night had moved the sand into isolated and random dips and banks. I swam out when she got closer and helped her up. I hugged her as hard as I could, relieved.

'Where is he? He went in after you, he hasn't come up.'

We were holding each other on the bank, scanning the water intently, looking for him.

'He's a strong swimmer, he'll be fine,' I said.

The set of waves cleared and he didn't appear. Each second that passed weighed more than the last.

'Where the fuck is he?' We were holding each other and Babe was starting to panic. When you're waiting for someone to come up for air, seconds are torment.

'I don't know.' I was scared too. I tried to keep my mind busy by scanning the water and imagining him looking refreshed and cold, but smiling.

Babe and I ran into the water. Our optimism had expired. *Teddy!*

I was thrashing around, trying to get some vision on where he was.

'*Babe*, I'm going to swim out,' I gestured. I was calling out to Teddy, and then I heard Babe. I couldn't see what was happening, so I imagined the worse. I started to swim back.

'*Wren!*' she ran over to a body. He was way back near a

sandbank, floating face down. The tide was dragging him along the beach, and out in a rip. I swam over to him. I was thigh high in the water but I managed to flip him over. His eyes were open. He was gasping for air. I wanted to feel his arms around me to make sure he was really alive, I wanted to make sure he hadn't drowned out there and that his air pipes were clutching at air.

'I can't move,' he screamed.

'Wren, don't touch him!'

'I can't move, I can't fucking move.'

'We can't move him too much.'

'We need to get him on the shore before the next set comes in.' We dragged him to the sand as best we could.

'I can't feel anything!' he screamed.

Babe ran to the house to call the ambulance. I stayed with him, brushing the sand out of his wet hair. His beautiful body was motionless; his eyes were darting around with fear.

'I'm fucked,' he kept repeating.

'Shhhh, you're not fucked, you're in shock. You're fine. Just try not to panic.'

It was as though life and colour had been dull before, but now everything was slowing down with raw technicolour I'd never seen before. His lips were shivering into indigo. I took my hoodie off and put it on top of his torso. Trying to offer him warmth from the cold water. His wet t-shirt had the stitching on the outside; he'd thrown it on inside-out in a rush. His black jeans were sticking to his body. Babe was running back now. We locked eyes and I tried not to be scared and tried to think of the moments I had bookmarked as ours for the taking. The ambulance would be on their way soon. His eyes were bloodshot from the salt water.

'I'm sorry.' He looked away the furthest his iris could go. I looked at him waiting. I sensed that something was coming, a question, a confession; he was finding the words or holding them in.

He shut his eyes and sobbed. I'd never seen a man sob like that. I touched his palm, motionless on the sand; I wanted to comfort him. I lay my head on his chest, I lay on the rise and fall of his breath; we wept together.

FOUR

The sea was angry the day the earth emerged from its rule. Once long ago according to the Popol Vuh, the sea came first. The fluid chrysalis fought to keep its bedrock intact, though terra firma came to form amongst rupturing clouds, violent enough to turn white and blue water, to black. Finally with impunity, ground was laid so that eventually, we could be created by the Gods to simply worship. The ocean was never meant for us. That same ancient ocean gave warning to us that day Babe and Teddy went in, we were not welcome to be part of its demonstration of force, she was trying to reclaim some of the earth she had lost before. The water visits me when I sleep. In my dreams it appears like golden scales, shallow and warm around my feet. Sometimes I feel the darkest gradients underneath from where I float, hiding something menacing. Once I was in La Libertad, El Salvador again, burying my toes in sand which looked primal and volcanic. Sometimes the waves are coming for me. We are mostly water but the materialisation of land separated us from our origins, and though we wanted to, we could never go back. We couldn't invoke water as ice now, nor ocean into snow.

I swore I'd never talk to myself about him, I'd always think of Teddy in the now because retrospect had the kind of sadness which could make me bitter. His eyes were closed and facing the afternoon sun upward, his face was of delight, he was enjoying the warmth.

'Do you mind if I have some of that?' I was eyeing off a tray of food he had refused to eat which consisted of one dry mound of mashed potatoes, a ladle of beef stroganoff which looked like slop but didn't smell too bad, and cup of orange juice. All accompanied by those small plastic cups of blue, red, and white pills.

'Yeah, you can have it.' He opened his eyes long enough to give me a little wink. 'Can you bring me sushi next time instead of a burger Wren. I don't want to get fat.' He smiled.

'I don't know why you hate this stuff so much, I love hospital food.' I took a mouthful of the mash and beef and grinned back at him.

'That's because you've never stayed in a hospital. This is what I eat three times a day, every day.' He had a point and he knew it so he scrunched his eyes up and I smoothed his hair lovingly to let him know he was right.

The truth be told, I hadn't eaten properly in a couple of days. I just snacked on fruit and the odd two-minute noodle packet. My bank account was running on empty; but I also started to see food as fuel and not a pleasure.

'Well, since you've eaten most of that,' he smiled, 'can I please have that mandarin?'

I grabbed it and held it in the ball of my palm and stabbed my fingernails into the porous, glossy skin. The oils burst into the air and laced the autumnal air with the smell of citrus. Teddy's face was still up toward the sun with his eyes closed.

'I love that smell,' he smiled big and wide to no one in particular. I placed a piece in his mouth, and he accepted it without opening his eyes; he just chewed and smiled, he let his mouth swing open for another piece.

Teddy had a fracture in the C5 section of his spinal cord. He was only able to move his arms slightly now and his head, of course. He finally opened his eyes, they were greener today, more so than usual. Today was a good day for him. He was lighter today. He touched my hand before I could feed him more fruit. A black tear landed on his white sheets, I tried to dry my eyes with the back of my finger, careful to not disturb any more makeup.

'Having a spinal cord injury is like having debris on the road after a storm. It's still there, it still works but because there's debris, the traffic can't flow through. We just have to find a way around it.'

I nodded as I sat back down and then proceeded to take mouthfuls of the cold mash. 'Do you want me to pull the skins off the segments? It tastes a hundred times better because you can feel all the little pieces inside the flesh of the mandarin and it pops in your mouth.' I didn't finish my sentence before I started actually doing it. I needed to keep myself busy; I didn't want to ruin his good day. It'd been a while since he smiled so much.

'Um, yeah, sure.'

I peeled it and tossed the clear casing of the mandarin on the tray, and put the open segments in his mouth. He snapped his head back at me with a creased brow and continued.

'So getting everything to work is just a matter of finding an alternative path, Ok Wren?' He was looking at me intently, I was looking at the mandarin skin drying on the tray; it looked like skin no longer needed and left behind. 'Fuck, you're right! I've never eaten it like that before. It's amazing. You gotta come round more.' He joked as I peeled another segment. I visited too much.

'You should stay. The girls are dropping in. You'll finally get to meet Agi!' He moved his hands in the air almost pleading. I couldn't meet them yet. The truth was I couldn't face them. The last time I'd heard Madeleine's voice she was shrill with panic and blaming Babe and I for 'This fucked up shit'. She blamed the drugs, the road trip, she blamed me.

'I've got to get going. I've got a job interview tomorrow. But I can maybe drop in after it and tell you how I didn't get the gig.'

'Okay, Wren.' He beamed, he often found my blunt cynicism amusing.

I decided to go see Babe. When I got to her place she was stuffing a cone-piece and Sayed was lounging on the couch next to her, his eyes looked bloodshot from afar, and he was going through every channel.

'Hey!' Babe said excitedly when she noticed I had used my key to get in. 'Let's get some food, I'm so hungry!'

Sayed and Babe had being getting high, for how long, I couldn't discern right away but the curtains were drawn, and the fog was drifting through, looking for air. This was their inertia, the tapping of their phones, the vacuous stare into the TV for hours. It only came out at night, that's when it was the most noticeable at least. Teddy's excruciating reality was always present and pushing me down places I didn't know, this all seemed so sad and pointless. In that moment, I had to leave even though I had just gotten there.

'Hey, where you going?' Babe's reaction was fast though her words were slightly slower. I stood there for a moment thinking.

After the accident Babe came to visit Teddy at the hospital. He was bound up, with the standard thin plastic tube coming in and out of his nose and veins. God knows where it all goes. He was in a brace and was bound to the bed. Most days there were at least five people in his room. The 'get well' cards had become so plentiful that Ness, a childhood best friend of his, had strung up some twine around the room and to each corner of the window to display all of them correctly. There were teddy bears and balloons too. Why the fuck a grown man would want such things in his room to begin with, I'll never understand. The flowers were replaced as soon as the corners of the petals began to brown. Death was not welcome in his room. It was shrine-like. The people came in droves to show support and love, and through their smiling teeth and their tears there was a sense of worship. It was too much of a circus for Babe.

'I'm ordering food for us, stay Wren, I haven't seen you for ages.' Babe took my standing there as reluctance, my mind was racing so I sat down.

Babe saw the hospital as a circus and it was. People who Teddy hadn't seen for years, some he didn't know anymore, they visited and in weeks they grew in numbers. They'd roll in packs, having once shared last names and old high-school timetables and places where they'd shared their stories about shit mid-management. I encountered more 'How do you know Teddy?' type questions more than I'd ever encountered. Sometimes I felt like I was being pulled into a competition of sorts, around who was closest to him and who knew him longest. I'd always get pushed to the back, or into the surrounding curtain which bordered his bed and have to wait out their idle chatter, their school night curfews before he and I would be alone again. There was a Facebook group for him; his face and his story was plastered everywhere on social media, there was a local news article. There was even a suitably patronising hashtag for him: #ourteddysjourney. Ness was the ringmistress of it all and I grew to know her better than I liked to. She had the spirit of a repressed childless soccer mum, an obsessive PR boss-pleaser. She was deeply overprotective of Teddy and she'd taken a dis-liking to me, she thought it was subtle, though it was palpable. She'd perverted his privacy and he let her get away with it under the guise of 'Oh that's just Ness'. If it wasn't all so tragic it would've been tragic! He was entombed by vigils and confes-sions, entwined in hospital-grade linen. Babe mentioned later she found it disturbing the way his eyes frantically followed voices around the room during conversation while he lay on his back motionless, as though he was the living dead. After that she never visited again, she couldn't even mention him unless I did. When I did make mention of Teddy she changed the subject, or turned the TV up, one day she left the room and closed her bedroom door when I insisted on talking about him. I waited for her to come out of her room for hours. When she finally opened the door she sat beside me and put her cold feet under my socks.

'Do you think everyone knows it was our fault?' she said. I said I hoped not.

'I can't stand this way you're living now Babe, I mean what's the point?'

'The point is,' She slurred, 'Kids don't do drugs.' Her and Sayed gave out little separate laughs.

'You shouldn't be getting high off your own supply Babe.'

'Why? I know I have the best shit.'

Babe once avoided drugs, she mentioned those government ads which showed women with open sores, toothless smiles and frantic eyes frightened her, they were the images of a modern witch, a woman hated, a woman hunted and scorned. They didn't stop her from going on benders with Sayed. It just meant she checked if her teeth were wobbly more regularly.

Babe squinted her eyes and watched me put my hands in her palms.

'I'm tired of this Babe.'

'You guys are fucking with my high. Remotes yours Babe.' Sayed left and threw the remote on the couch next to me. The TV blasted with some blonde reality show woman.

'You have to stop seeing him,' she said, 'He should just focus on his life now, not me or you. I mean what good would it do him to have you there?'

'I can believe you'd say that but why do you have to mean it?'

I got up and left. She didn't call after me, not that I expected her too from her drug haze. She was right. My visits to go see him had gotten more and more frequent.

Teddy had moved into a spinal rehabilitation clinic, after a while of being at the hospital, after the crowds had feathered out to less visits.

I got into the routine of visiting Teddy in the morning. That way I'd avoid running into Maddie and his father, who was usually drunk. Sometimes I'd watch him do his exercises on the machines which moved his legs for him. The water exercises where his favourite, but nothing made him look more fragile. Being waded through water by a woman was one of the few things that could revert you back to infancy.

I even managed to stop crying at the drop of a hat. My mum said it was my way of mourning a part of our lives and I shouldn't be afraid of it. I got offered a job as an account manager at a Melbourne boutique agency. It was part of my contract that they'd allow time for me to go to Award School to pursue copywriting full-time, it was something. I told Teddy, and he was glad for me, but I saw his eyes start to drift away as I spoke about the opportunity more.

We'd gotten closer than we ever had before. Maybe helping him right now wasn't helping either of us but I couldn't stop. We'd started to create our own language and we used shorthand, like skidding when we wanted to go for a walk. His sick sense of humour had done something so few people could ever make me do: laugh and cry at the same time. I stopped wearing makeup and started to wear more colour, I sought it out everywhere not just on fabric, I felt excited on the 505 bus at the thought of seeing him, and each time I walked up that grassy knoll I quickened my steps to almost running. He'd let me ride with him on his chair through the grounds, at first I was afraid of hurting him but he retorted that he survived a weekend with Babe and I, so nothing could kill him now.

The nurses at the clinic became family his family, sharing private jokes, he asked about their kid's by name. When we wanted privacy from their prying eyes like teens from parents, we'd kiss under the stairs which lead down to the paddock. We'd sit there when it rained, and feeling close to him would stir elation. My gratitude for him had been prospering the way ivy grew on barren walls or blank paper for William Carlos Williams' "The Ivy Crown". It was rebelling against the very nature of its terrain. Its chosen path was both audacious and unwinding. Gifting gravity a wreath of defiance to show life.

'Heya Teddy, what's on the menu for lunch?'

'Why? Do you want it!?'

'I brought you sushi, fatty,' I smiled.

'It's actually spag bowl today. So fuck it coz I'm a sucker for the occasional saucy carb.'

'Right, that's your favourite. Okay cool, I'll eat the sushi.' I saw the pasta sitting there, he usually had to wait to eat it because the nurse could only feed one inpatient at a time. I liked feeling useful to him and I liked having him to myself.

'Want me to do it?'

'Yeah, give the ol' girls bit of a break why don't cha,' he smiled.

We took our lunch in the courtyard. There was a fountain in the middle, like the one at his café full of greenery.

Maddie and Teddy decided to sell the cafe and buy a smaller business down the track maybe, but for now it would fund Teddy's needs. It had sold for a considerable amount. But his recuperation was expensive. His new electronic chair was custom built and retailed at $12,000.

I put paper napkins all over his shirt to protect him from the sauce I was no doubt about to paint him with. I rolled the biggest spiral of pasta around the fork as I could. He braced himself. He knew I was being cheeky. It got everywhere.

'Fucks sake, Wren!' He tried to laugh through the mouthful of pasta.

'Sorry,' as I munched on a rainbow roll. After lunch we went to his room. A room he shared with a much older gentleman who sometimes had the odd family member visit, they were always just as old as him. I ran my fingers through his hair trying to style it; it was too long and it fell in the wrong places. My eyes moved away from his hair and connected with his glassy eyes.

'I would've drowned if you didn't see me when you did.' I didn't know what to say. 'When I was under that water I thought, "That's it for me." Then you came.' I didn't let him finish, I didn't want to. So I kissed him long and gently while my eyes rested on a picture he had on his nightstand, it was us together sitting by the Bougainvillea in the courtyard, it had my cursive on it, and it read *I see you*. I tried to picture what would run through my mind when I looked at this picture in the future. Maybe we'd be in a different city, I'd have different hair, he'd be walking, maybe, and we would laugh about this hard time in our lives when we fell in love, just before things changed for the better. Teddy loved me with a conviction that was always his own. His love was abundant because his deepest happiness was when I gave him a chance to express it. He didn't have walls built around him because it wasn't built on ego or entitlement. He wanted to make me feel safe enough for long enough for me to show him who I was. He was just like that. I always hoped to be loved like that, with understanding and kindness.

We kissed for hours under the cement staircase which looked out to a road and field. We chatted about us, music, our book, we were both reading Marquez; we talked about love and how it manifested in many forms. He talked about his new challenges and fatherhood. He revealed he also lost a child too, with Maddie. We kissed and talked till the nurses started calling out his name to go get his medicine.

'What are your plans for tonight?'

'I'm going to see Babe.'

'Wow, really? You haven't seen her for a while.' It was true. I hadn't seen her for a couple months. She had completely isolated herself, and I decided to give her space to deal with whatever she had to deal with. She had finally contacted me and wanted to know if I was free to hang.

'Yeah, it sounded like she had news, so I'm bit scared. You never know with her... I miss her.'

'Can you tell her she should cut the crap and come visit me? I miss her too.'

'I'll do my best.'

I met Babe at a converted cellar, now a pub called The Old Growler down a staircase in Darlinghurst. She didn't look good. Her hair was growing at different stages. It looked like, at some point, she had taken to it with some scissors herself. She was thinner than ever and her eyes were almost protruding out of her face. She reminded me of a forgotten statue buried under the rubble from a civilisation people now could only dream of. Her eyes had no light; she was completely overtaken by her surroundings.

'Lawrence!' She seemed glad to see me and fell into me for a hug.

'Hey, how are you guys?'

We sat down. Sayed was colder than usual, maybe a touch catty, which made me awkward.

'Well, let's throw a couple cocktails down then, shall we?' Teddy was calling me; he usually had his phone next to his hand. He had a nurse attach a device which could activate Siri to call and text. He was calling me from his bed but I'd call him back in a bit.

We drank till the crowd started to thin out and leave, including Sayed. Babe grabbed my hand.

'This is going to sound dramatic but I need to go away for a bit.' She was drunk, so I had to listen carefully. 'I don't know when I'm coming back or if I'll ever come back.' She drank half her glass of wine in one long sip. I saw that Teddy sent a text but I didn't open it. I refocused on Babe.

'Pssh, stop being so cryptic, Babe. You're scaring me,' there was something different about her. She seemed more womanly but not in that beautiful way a woman can come to accomplish. It was a dull resignation she was emitting and I suppose that came off as a type of maturity but really it was her looking beaten.

'I'm sorry.' She put her head in her hands. 'Sayed is putting in for me to get help.' She took a moment as if she wasn't done with her confession and was only starting. 'It's taken over my life, Wren. The only reason I know this now is because I've run out of money and I can barely function without it. I've done some fucked up stuff to get it but the worse thing is I've stolen from some shitty people and I've heard that they're looking for me now.' She was crying but it appeared to be out of genuine fear. 'I've made a fucking mess, actually. I don't know how to fix it so I have to get clean and hopefully they don't find me. I'll probably try going back to my family after, if they'll have me back.' Teddy was calling again.

'And if they don't want you back?' I asked concerned. She just shook her head. 'Babe, what did you do to bring all this on?'

'It's the guy that I get my shit from. I owe him money, he knows I smoked most of the stuff and he's pissed. The only reason why he let me sell ice was because I wasn't a fan, that's all gone to shit now. I'm still short even though I marked up my prices.'

The story Babe was telling me felt like moving pictures. I was watching this conversation outside of myself as though I was watching a Buñuel film. I knew what was happening: Babe was in deep shit. How could I not foresee this? How could I have not been there to help her avoid it?

'I'm sorry I haven't been there for you or Teddy. I haven't been there for anyone, not even myself.' She slurred her words. I embraced her.

'Come stay with me on the coast. Don't take it on all by yourself Babe. I'm here.' She nodded with tears in her eyes.

'You can't help me now but I love you for always trying.' She was drunk and she hugged me again, I could feel her bones hugging me back and asking for a meal or warmth.

'Love you too, kid.'

'Sayed is taking me tomorrow, I'm glad we got to say bye to each other and hang, even if it's just for a little while.'

I watched her walk off. Sometimes I wondered if she was real or a composite figure I had created to feel less alone. She belonged to the lost little girls that existed in the cultural ether... Were we created in their image or did we create them? She was my oldest friend. She was a chameleon, an evolutionary trait made for people with no providence for learning about the self. She had to be, because of her puritan parents and well, the world. Sometimes she was so hard to see that I'd forget her, who the real Babe was. Then she'd eat food over the sink, or try to adopt stray cats which weren't stray, or be barefoot with torn-off jeans in the winter so she could show off her best assets, her legs, which were like sawn-off shotguns. She was like all of us, using drugs or people to numb the hunger of loneliness, using sex as shorthand for love. The trouble is love was self-immolating, whereas sex is self-serving; it'll never do, it was never enough.

I felt nostalgia because part of me felt like this would be the end of something special between us, she was gone and I couldn't help her. Something was changing and suffering always followed change. I tried not to envision Babe going to money lents, throwing cigarette butts in neon puddles outside the golden mile, haunting run-down bars, doing more illegal hand-shakes. Refusing to die, but also refusing to live. I hoped that wouldn't be the case. I thought about her alone in her room, looking out to the stars and wondering if anyone would remember her out there. I hoped she would think of me and know that I was also wondering the same thing somewhere about myself, and that I was thinking of her.

I hailed a cab. I looked at my phone. 2:45 am. I was drunk but I wanted to be near him, so I told the cabbie to go west; to Teddy. He never slept with his window locked. I could easily reach over and swing the latch from the outside. He wanted to see me, he'd been calling all night while I was busy with Babe.

I reached under the window and lifted it slowly. I got the cab to drop me down the way so I could creep up. He was in bed and I could see the white of his eyes in the dark.

'You scared me,' he whispered.

'Sorry.' I was squeezing through the window. I knew he was grinning, I knew he was happy to see me breaking the rules, same as we always did.

'Can you scratch my nose?' I ran my finger nails over his nose hoping to hit the spot. 'What are you doing here, crazy girl?'

'I wanted to see you.'

'Come here,' I came closer as he commanded.

'I'm getting into bed with you, give me a sec.' I struggled to get on but I eventually curled up next to him.

'What did you do tonight?' We were whispering and through the torch on my phone I could see the beautiful white of his porcelain teeth and his eyes registering my face.

'Drinks. I have so much to tell you.' Our kisses always started out as playful pecks, but deepened into lustful mouthfuls of each other. Between these mouthfuls I could feel the ache of sexual desire in me. I hated feeling that. I wanted it to go away.

'I want you so bad,' I whispered between our kisses.

'I want you too.'

I lifted the sheet between us. He was nude. I saw his neck, his well-defined chest, his flat and muscular stomach, his penis, flaccid and pink resting on a nest of brown hair.

'He doesn't belong to me anymore.' He seemed embarrassed. 'He's been given away to science.' There was a clear tube through it somehow. He was looking at it now too.

'I'm sorry.' I'd never seen medical paraphernalia near a penis; it shocked me for a moment. I put the sheet down and put my arm over his chest.

'Wren, I could never give you everything I would want to give you.'

'No one can, that's okay.'

'You would be with someone who couldn't make love to you?'

'Yes. We'll figure something out.' I was intrigued at how passionate I was about this. My mind started to move through professions, names, situations that can somehow help us.

'We can only give what we can give. Wren this life shouldn't be yours too. I wouldn't want that for you.'

I put my fingers on his mouth. 'Let's not talk about this please.' He kept going.

'I'm begging you Teddy.' I was openly weeping now so he stopped talking.

We eventually started to fell asleep.

When I woke up I realised I dreamt about Teddy. I tried to reimagine the dream. We were in our best clothes walking down a street and the ground started to move. Teddy said it was an earthquake and we both needed to get to a clearing. All I remember is watching him climb up this rocky hill and the further he went up the more violently the earth moved. He kept saying to stay there and he'd check to see if it was safe for me to join him, but it never was and I woke up. His eyes were open and I smiled to him. He didn't smile back.

'I had a dream you walked last night. You were wearing that badly fitted suit like the one you use to wear to job interviews. You know that suit that made you look scrawny but handsome?'

He laughed, I cracked his bad mood.

'And poor. That's how you described me then, scrawny and poor. Wren, I think you should take that job.'

'I fucking knew you were going to say this Teddy, I knew it!' I snapped my body up and was crying again, looking down at him lying on his back. 'I won't take it. You know the hundred reasons why!'

'That's fine. I don't want to be one of them, though. Can we please both be selfish and try to be happy for one another?'

'What does that mean?'

'Wren, I can't even listen to music anymore, it reminds me of what I used to be. I heard a Motown song one night and I cried myself to sleep because I knew that song will always remind me of when I could walk.'

'I thought you wanted to be with me too Teddy?'

'I do but Wren, but look at me.' He sensed I looked away. This angered him. 'Look at me!' He didn't whisper it this time. His eyes were desperately angry and drowning under his tears. 'I can't even shit alone anymore. Will you stick your fingers up my ass to help me shit? Will you do that for me every morning? Will you bathe me, turn me so I don't get bed sores, will you love me after all that? Will you come see me when I have to go to an old folks home because I can't be cared for anywhere else? Or will we live together in a house of ramps and a daughter not your own, and an ex who blames you? All I'd do is need you... Could you bear that for the rest of your life? How could you ever stay in love with me? That's no fucking life. It is mine though... I fucked up. You have to go, the nurses will be in soon and they'll know you snuck in to see me.'

'Tell me you don't love me. Say it, Teddy!'

'That's not the point, Wren. I'll always love you. I'll even be there for you when you marry someone else. Invite me to your wedding and I'll drop everything to come and see you; to come see you happy. For now, please... you have to go. But don't come back here. It'll fucking kill me if you do Lawrence, I swear it will, I won't survive saying goodbye to you again'. My face was in my hands. I thought of the man next to Teddy in the hospital ward all those months ago. He'd come off a push bike on a hill while riding with his daughters. The nurses eventually put padded safety gear on him to prevent him from smashing his head against the metal bed frame and medical equipment at night. He was tormented by his life now. His wife explained the danger of suicide for people who had to learn to live with disability due to an accident. She endured the cruelest names from him when he had his fits. She was always so kind to me, like we were both just women wanting to love despite a tragic outcome. She spoke to me about the pain and accepting that this hurt was a part of their way of life for now. Sometimes he'd be OK, sometimes the lack of pain was too much. I believe her stories were hidden messages for me to get out. I was still young and not all was over. I wanted to endure it for us but I didn't know if I had it in me to weather those storms. The sorrow of having him, but not the way he intended me to have him, was too deep to bear. He deserved more than doubt.

I forced my eyes to capture him, in that moment. There are such few things I love and all those things I'd give away, if it meant Teddy had a better story. I got up off his bed. I placed my manuscript next to him, just near enough so he can direct a nurse to it if he needed.

'This is yours now. It's about us.' I kissed him on the forehead, and then I left through the window. When I reached the other side of the glass I heard him crying. I tried to see him through the frosted glass in an attempt to take it back or just see him. I wanted to go back in but I felt the desperation in his voice when he promised he couldn't handle saying good bye again. So instead, I sat in the dirt and wept too.

I eventually got myself to the train station, so I could get home. An old university friend was letting me stay in her spare room on the coast. There were clouds clawing inland from a tempest I saw brewing on the shore. The clouds were pushing welts of rain across the train window. I imagined the garden pinwheel waiting to greet me at the front yard. I wondered if Teddy meant what he said: if he'd always love me. In the grand waltz of the hours, choreographed carefully between the amnesiac sun and the moon, does anyone ever have the luxury of time to know anyone, let alone to love them? Your fate is sealed and in the case of Teddy, Babe and I, it'll likely be an unkind one in which the world will consume us before we can truly love. Saturn would crunch us like ungrateful children; leaving us to reach out and try to find one another in the dark; leaving us in the dirty, cut, black hair of God's blue basin.

The beautiful brutality that lies within Gerii Pleitez's words dares you to flinch.

The daughter of El Salvadorean political dissidents who fled a bloody civil war, she discovered her art growing up amongst the streets of Western Sydney and went on to study writing at Wollongong University.

Gerii is the founder of Kara Sevda Press and what you are holding is the imprint's first published book.

www.karasevdapress.com
Instagram - @oohgigi
Twitter - @geriipleitez

Kara Sevda Press is a fiercely independent publisher from Naarm
(Melbourne), Australia. Our focus is on finding and empowering literary
voices from females of colour which have otherwise been deemed
commercially unviable by the literary establishment.

www.karasevda.com
@karasevdapress

·

www.ingramcontent.com/pod-product-compliance
Lightning Source LLC
Chambersburg PA
CBHW071131100726
47908CB00008B/2571